THE BUDDING
OF
PATATKURAPKI

BY

A. UMAZ

ISBN-13: 978-0692391280
ISBN-10: 0692391282

Published in Cooperation with **Helios  Press**

An imprint of IACP/Co-oPress

www.co-opress.org
Printed in the USA

Prologue

The retreat of the ice sheets and shelves and the thawing of the permafrost brought changes both good and bad. On the good side, continental plate that had been covered in excess of 10 millennia is increasingly exposed, thus becoming available for human exploitation. These regions are found to be rich in mineral and hydrocarbon and easily become the source of conflict. Adjacent nations quickly lay claim to these areas, and as quickly challenge the claims of their neighbors. As yet no "hot wars" have erupted, but the chilling effect upon international relations certainly promotes many a "cold war."

In the northern hemisphere vast stretches of North America, Greenland, Scandinavia, Northern Europe and Asia now lay exposed. The melting Arctic ice sheet has opened waterways and made exploration of the northern continental shelves possible. In the southern hemisphere retreating ice sheets and shelves have given access to the Antarctic continent and its vast, unexplored wealth.

The retreat of the ice has not come without a price. Nearly 30% of the Earth's population has been displaced by rising waters, a much greater number than any of the last century's predictions. By 2XXX it was realized that basic errors in calculation and understanding had caused estimates to be woefully low. Now, nearly 100 years later, the price is being paid for those errors. One critical error was in calculating the rebound effect on continental plates as the ice overburden lifted. Rebounding in Antarctica and the northern continental plates resulted in continental subsidence at lower latitudes, so that as sea levels rose, mid-latitude and tropical coastal elevations sank. Another miscalculation was the all too often predicted salvation through an "induced ice age" resulting from a slowing or halting of the oceans' thermohaline circuit. Instead, the rapidity of the melt coupled with the difference in density of fresh and salt water has resulted in a rapid dispersal of a layer of freshwater over the entire surface of the oceans, aided by increased winds as planetary air flows have accelerated in response to rising temperatures. The thermohaline circuit has persisted against all predictions, while the freshwater layer atop it, being less dense, has expanded beyond expectations. The exodus of populations from coastal regions as waters rise is an ongoing crisis, resulting in a multitude of regional conflicts as the immigrants put pressure on interior populations.

One of the least appreciated but increasingly problematic results of this climactic change, as Earth regresses to environmental conditions that have not existed for hundreds of millennium, if not millions of years, is the resuscitation of microbes and other organisms to which our species has no defense and with which we cannot easily cohabitate. Certain primitive algae whose metabolites are toxic to humans have now become so profligate that the atmosphere is rife with their spore so that it is a constant struggle just to maintain safe drinking water. Other bacterial and viral elements of novel genetics have been reintroduced into the environment causing new diseases to appear so rapidly that medical science is nearly overwhelmed by the challenge. And yet, for all this misery, the species endures, and in some small ways advances. We take our losses and adjust, with the certain faith that a new equilibrium will be established. As a medical doctor and evolutionary biologist, I for one find the new paradigm full of challenge and inspiration. In particular, I have been privileged to participate in a discovery so profound that until now it has been sequestered by governments and the scientific community. Many still dispute the findings and subject those of us certain of our results to vilification and professional ridicule. This inquisition notwithstanding, I am compelled to share with my fellow man the nature of this discovery and its implications in our past and for our future.

J. D. Bander, MD PhD
January 21, 2XXX

CHAPTER 1

The entire of the North American continent has been forced into a necessary but often fragile union in response to the exigencies of climate change. As populations retreat inland and northward, greater pressure for resources falls upon the central regions of Canada and the United States. The retreating ice and thawing permafrost to the north now provide a new frontier, inviting a whole host of pioneers to venture forth in hopes of improving their lives. Like so many now tired of the constant haggling over diminishing resources in the central regions, with the enthusiastic promotion of my teenage children and eventual consent of my dear wife, we booked passage on the Hudson Bay transport H.M.V. Nunavut, bound for the province of the same name. Several large population centers have developed on the north shore of the bay, where doctors and educators are in general demand. As I am qualified in both categories I was confident of finding employment.

The transport on which we traveled was primarily engaged in delivering modules to the frontier. These modules ranged from smallish residential models, to vast industrial units composed of multiple modules. During the overnight voyage I availed myself of the opportunity to examine some of the more accessible modules stacked on the main deck. One particular grouping of units whose interiors were partially visible through the plastic wrappings of their open ends would obviously constitute a laboratory when assembled. Upon closer inspection I saw they were tagged CBT, a symbol I was familiar with. It stood for Culverson BioTech, an up and coming company in the field of bioengineering. They had made a name for themselves by creating varieties of food grains and livestock that thrived in the regions of thawed permafrost, where the extreme slant of the Sun's rays delivered greatly reduced energy. Low light photosynthetic plants and high food to weight gain livestock were essential for successful agriculture in the high latitudes.

I had put my cupped hands to the surface of the plastic, and thus shading my eyes was trying to get a better view of the interior of one of the units, when I was somewhat startled to see a human form within advancing in my direction. I stepped back just as a hand tugged at the plastic sheet's edge, pulling it back to reveal the face of a pleasant looking young fellow.

"Hello." His smile indicated he took no offense at my nosiness. "Would you like to look around?" He held back the sheet and indicated that I should enter.

"Well…yes.   I'm a physician and bio-evolutionist and, well, a laboratory calls to me like home!" I returned his smile.

"Oh, by the way, I'm Davison Culverson." He extended his hand.

"Pleased to me you.   J.D. Bander, here." The surprise on my face brought his next remark.

"I'm not THE Davison Culverson!" he said with chuckle. "That would be my father."

"Ah…I thought you looked a bit young, or extremely well preserved." My humor did not go unappreciated.

"What have we got here," I queried, observing that the rows of equipment were obviously thermocyclers, used for the amplification of DNA. "Looking to do some PCR on a rather large scale, are we?"

Again he chuckled. "Yes, as a matter of fact. The deeper strata in the thawed permafrost ought to yield some interesting samples of extremely old and well preserved DNA."

"I understand that there have been some novel and rather dangerous virions and bacteria unearthed at some of the mining and prospecting sites." The new diseases – or should I say very ancient ones – were part of my motivation for heading to the frontier.

"Yes. Another of our goals is to identify the DNA in these pathogens so that we can engineer preventions and cures." His gaze narrowed in contemplation, and then suddenly expanded with anticipation. "Say, you aren't already committed in the territory are you? We're always looking for help."

I had not anticipated a job offer when I had begun my evening's stroll, but its sudden manifestation seemed the most natural of occurrences. "Well…no. That is, I am not committed. Just heading north with the family looking for opportunity. If you're making an offer, I'll accept!"

"Good!" Culverson beamed a smile. "Let's settle things in the morning over coffee, before we disembark."

We shook hands. He escorted me to the modules open end and once again pulled back the plastic curtain as I exited.

"See you in the morning!" He seemed quite pleased with himself.

"Yes, in the morning." I was quite pleased with myself as well.

CHAPTER 2

Passenger accommodations onboard the H.M.V. Nunavut were rather spartan. Our compartment consisted of two sets of bunked beds fit into alcoves opposite each other. The narrow isle between them terminated at a small desk set below a rather large porthole. All storage was relegated to draws under the bunks. The quarters had obviously been designed for crew, but when the demand for passenger berths erupted and fares skyrocketed, shipping companies found it more profitable to berth their crews in container units on deck and use the existing crew quarters for passengers. As a result, the head and the galley were common to all passengers.

The voyage from New Fort Rupert at the south of James Bay (the old Fort Rupert has long been submerged) to New Baker Lake (same story) was well over 1000 km. But the H.M.V. Nunavut was a hydroplane ship and clipped along at nearly 40 knots, easily making the trip in 24 hours. Even with the frequent 4 to 6 meter swells the ship's hull only graced the tops of the waves, and stabilized by the deep running wings of the hydroplanes, the voyage was quite pleasant.

I returned to our cabin just as the evening mess bell rang, and quickly thronged by my hungry spouse and offspring, we made our way aft through the narrow passages towards the galley, soon joined by the other passengers and off-watch crew sliding skillfully down the ladders from upper decks.

Evident from their demeanor and apparent bachelorhood, the majority of our fellow passengers seemed to be prospectors, or at least men headed to work in the mining fields just north of the Canadian Shield. New trends of nickel and copper ores along with platinum, palladium, silver and gold had been discovered beneath the thawing tundra. As has happened so often in the past the lure of riches, or at least steady employment, has attracted a plethora of adventurous souls – mine not withstanding!

During the course of a rather raucous dinner, I overheard many a conversation premised in the rumors that always abound among those pursuing good fortune. One young fellow announced quite authoritatively that miners were in such demand that they could expect to be paid and to live as well any rich man. Another immediately countered saying that technicians were what was demanded, and that laborers fared no better in the north than did those in the lower latitudes. Yet another began a tale of strange maladies no doctor could cure and curses laid down by native shaman in revenge for the rape of their land. I was particularly interested in the talk of strange maladies as part of my reasoning for the current expedition was to observe firsthand, study, and if possible cure new diseases if they were in fact occurring. I listened more closely as the young man expounded on his marginally credible speculations.

"Heard it straight from the mouth of a fellow that was there! Diggin' in the hard rock. Come across veins – and I don't mean veins of ore – I mean like *human* veins – pulsing, that bleed when you cut them! Some bleed stuff that'll make you sick enough to die; some bleed stuff that'll burn you like an acid! He'd hit 'em both, and the scares to show. Burned all down the side of his face and neck, and still weak and barely able to eat. I saw him in Fort Rupert – he looked like walkin' death!"

Of course, he was immediately set upon by the skeptics, who ridiculed his naiveté and as quickly offered their own explanations. One reckoned it was gas from the decaying tundral mat; another reckoned it was acid, but not running in veins, but percolating down through crevices in the rock, another by-product of the decaying matter above. I, of course, accepted both hypotheses as possible, with the addition of strange virions and bacteria long trapped in the frozen earth added to the mix. They were all hypotheses I hoped to test.

CHAPTER 3

Early the next morning Culverson sent a message around to our cabin asking me to join him for coffee in the laboratory unit. I dressed quickly, and upon emerging on the main deck saw the low coastline and inlet leading to New Baker Lake. We would be several hours arriving yet, so I hurried to my appointment. As it was early May, the morning breeze still had a considerable bite at these latitudes though no snow or ice could be seen anywhere. Culverson had a deckhand standing by to open the plastic curtain and usher me in. I ducked inside quickly.

It was obvious that Culverson was making his berth in the laboratory. The climate units and lighting were working, and he had engineered a rather ingenious double boiler apparatus out of available glassware and tubing and was in the process of brewing a thick, rich espresso. He even had a wand for frothing. Aware of my entrance, he offered a "Good morning!" with his back turned to me, intent on finishing his task. A boiling flask quickly produced the steam that forced the water through the ground coffee, which he collected in two small beakers. Adding a small amount of cream of sugar, he expertly frothed the mixtures, and turning slowly with the hot brew offer me one of the ersatz coffee cups, indicating that I should hold it by the rim to avoid the heat of the contents. I sipped carefully at the sumptuous froth as he began.

"We'll be in port in an hour or so, and I'll be busy most of the day supervising the off-loading of these units, so I thought we could take a few moments this morning to discuss the terms of your employment." He slurped at the tasty foam and then continued.

"You're just the sort we're looking for up here – multi-talented and obviously with a sense of adventure." His eyes gleamed with mischievousness. "We've got a lot of challenges facing us up here – as many bad as good. Right now we're nearly overwhelmed by the bad!" He fixed his gaze on the remaining brew in his beaker as if trying to read from its contents, like an oracle examining the entrails of a bird or a shaman interpreting the patterns in cast bones.

"The mining companies are footing the bill for our transport and set-up costs. They've got a lot at stake here. There have been some outbreaks of new and as yet unidentified pathogens that have got the locals spooked, and some of the men afraid to go into the mines. The mines are mostly automated of course, but in the end it takes a man underground to make the right choices and make the operation profitable. Of course, you've probably heard some of the rumors...." He looked at me inquisitively.

"As a matter of fact I have! Just last night in the galley a young fellow was going on about such things…human like veins in rock; acid blood; toxic gasses. I expect those are highly exaggerated depictions of the real events. Still, you could see it had a chilling effect on the rest of the passengers."

Culverson listened very intently, then responded immediately: "Yes, yes. Just what I'm talking about! We've got to get in there and find out what's going on before a panic sets in. Nothing is more contagious – or dangerous – than the spread of ignorance!"

Culverson raised his now mostly empty beaker to me and raising his eyebrows asked by gesture if I would care for more. I was already buzzing from the jolt of sugar and caffeine and declined with an adamant side to side shake of my head. He beamed back in pleasure at this assertion of the potency of his brew.

"To business then… We already have a small operation set up on Garry Lake, in the Kivalliq Region, but we're going to need a much larger facility nearer the new deposits so we're taking this equipment on to New Baker Lake. When we make dock I'll have a hover craft waiting to take you and your family over to Garry Lake. There are accommodations there – everything you'll need, just not the Hilton! My man down there will get you acquainted with what we've got going on. As soon as we get the new labs up and running, I'll send for you. Any questions!"

Culverson's manner had turned quite abrupt and perfunctory. It was obvious his mind had turned to the tasks ahead. I had questions, though.

"Mr. Culverson, before we part, I would like to ask a few questions!"

"Oh…about salary?"

"No…No! About what you've found already; what you're looking for!"

"Ah! Yes! How thoughtless of me. A million wheels turning…" Culverson nodded toward a nearby table covered with charts. I followed him there.

"We've been working with and for the mining companies since the beginning of these new projects. Everyone accepted the possibility there might be unusual consequences in disturbing soil that's been frozen for anywhere from 10 to 100 thousand years. The new ore trends are shallow, but still, removing the overburden requires displacing millions upon millions of cubic meters of soil – soil that formed millions of years ago, and has been frozen since the last glacial period. A lot has happened since then." Davison Culverson delivered one of those Mona Lisa like half smiles to indicate the irony of his remark.

He continued: "We anticipated the possibility of complications – the release of unusual compounds; perhaps ancient pathogens. We did not count of the certainty of it…the compounding complications."

All the while Culverson had been leaning with hands spread on the table, staring down at the charts. With circular motions of a finger he indicated regions to the northeast of Garry Lake and north of New Baker Lake.

"Here…and here! These were the first two places to report anomalies. First there were some inhalation casualties and chemical burns reported by drilling crews in the pits. Then, after blasting there were reports of toxic clouds and acidic vapor by the removal crews. But most troubling of all have been the reported cases, some now verified, of a sort of dementia that sets in. The first case was reported by an exploration crew just here." Culverson indicated a small area about midway between the earlier indicated mining sites. One crew abandoned their equipment and were found several days later wandering aimlessly. Examinations found no cause, and when interviewed, the men could not remember what had happened." Culverson raised his head and looked at me. He sighed. "So…that's where we're at!"

"Will I get a chance to speak with these men?" My physician's side took precedence over the bio-evolutionist.

"Of course! Get settled in over at Garry Lake. All the files are there. I'll have the men sent down for medicals and you can question them then. The new labs will be up and running in a couple of weeks and then will have everything moved up here." He turned to me and smiled.

"And I promise better accommodations!…Not the Hilton, of course!"

Just as he finished his remarks, the H.M.V. Nunavut sounded her horn, indicating that she was entering the inlet.

"I'd best get back to my cabin. We're traveling light, but still, there are things to do before we arrive." In acknowledgement Culverson turned back to his charts. I departed quietly, filled with anticipation!

CHAPTER 4

After returning to the cabin I told my wife and children of my meeting with Culverson and the prospect of my new employment. My wife was delighted. Though she had not shown it overtly, it is in the nature of wives and mothers to worry when their nest is uncertain. I could see that the fact we would immediately have a home and income relieved her burden. As for the children, I had hinted at the mysterious occurrences I would be investigating, which ignited their imaginations. Both having inherited my scientific bent, their speculations flowed freely.

"Aliens!" my son blurted out unrestrainedly.

My daughter, being a bit more of the romantic, offered: "Native spirits, called forth by an Inuit medicine man. At last, science and supernatural come face to face!" She was pleased with her assessment, and smiled broadly.

"Gosh, this is gonna be like a science fiction movie!" my son concluded, also well pleased with himself.

The two walked shoulder to shoulder sharing speculations and theories as we made our way down the vessels gangway to the dock. My wife chuckled and commented:

"At last! Something in common! Maybe this is going to be a better move than I anticipated." She smiled and took my arm. I was pleased – an auspicious beginning!

I did not see Davison Culverson as we disembarked the vessel at New Baker Lake, but true to his word a hover craft idled at dockside waiting to take us aboard.

The captain of the hover craft and his two native crewmen relieved us of our luggage and ushered us aboard. The craft's cabin was amazingly spacious, with the cockpit forward, a small galley and table mid ship, with a well stuffed, curved couch set beneath a panoramic window that constituted the back bulkhead of the cabin. A small ladder divided the couch which indicated a passage to compartments below, probably the engine room and crew quarters.

Without delay the captain but the vessel underway. Though well accounted the cabin was not so well sound-proofed. As the turbines and props spooled up and the craft levitated on the cushion of air trapped within it skirts, the subsequent roar made ordinary communication impossible. Noting our distress, the captain motioned to headsets hanging on pegs in the ladder well. Securing a pair each for myself, my wife, and the children, we donned them quickly. The captain's voice came through perfectly.

"Welcome aboard the Caribou. Make yourselves comfortable. Anuun will make some beverages and get you anything else you need from the galley. Anyone care for some whale blubber?" The captain chuckled at his own humor. "No?!" He feigned disappointment. "Well then, it'll take us about 2 hours to get to Garry Lake. You can nap on the couches if you like, but use the seatbelts. The head is down the ladder to the right."

With that he turned abruptly to the cockpit, and relieving his other crewman of the controls began to pilot the craft. We took places along the couch, and turning our attentions to the retreating vista out the back glass watched as the miles passed under us. It was at once a bleak and yet intimidating scene. As New Baker Lake slid below the horizon to our stern all that remained was an interminable distance alternated only by myriad ponds like small mirrors laid upon the now greening mat of the tundra. Historically beyond the tree line because of temperature, the warming climate now permitted the planting of large plantations of hybrid conifers but there were none yet in this particular region.

The drone and vibration of machinery and the unaltering landscape had a hypnotic effect on all of us. Soon we dozed on the couch. I can only speculate as to the dreams of others, but for myself my dreams now opened up a great, black cleft in the green felt of the tundra from which issued all manner of demons who encircled me, absorbing me into their throng and thence whirling through ever increasingly incredible and terrifying terrains. My troubled sleep was only interrupted by a sudden deceleration and sinking as we arrived at our destination and the craft settled once again to earth. I awoke somewhat disoriented and troubled by my dreams, but I put them aside and prepared to embark on the next step in the adventure.

CHAPTER 5

As Davison Culverson had suggested, the accommodations at Garry Lake were not the Hilton! The Culverson Laboratories and Compound consisted of a half dozen well weathered modules circling a collection of storage tanks, the area crisscrossed with the tracks of vehicles whose routes had not yet coalesced into a well-defined road.

As we exited the hover craft we were greeted by an enthusiastic young man whose countenance carried a note of familiarity. He introduced himself, and the mystery was solved:

"Hello. I'm Benson Culverson. You must be Dr. Bander…and Mrs. Bander." He turned slightly toward my wife and punctuated his greeting with the hint of bow. Before I could inquire, my question was answered.

"Davison is my uncle. We're a family run operation." He smiled again, proudly.

"If you'll follow me I'll show you to your quarters. Once you get settled in, we can get started."

The young man was every bit as intense as his uncle. He motioned for two approaching figures to take our meager luggage, then together our small entourage headed for the nearest module.

We entered into a common area that served as kitchen, dining and recreation hall. From there he led us to a narrow hallway centered in the right wall that mirrored a similar passage in the left wall. Noticing my appraisal, he offered: "Those are my quarters to left. Hope you will find these sufficient, and maybe even comfortable." He grinned apologetically.

A pair of doors penetrated the side walls each side of the corridor, with a slightly larger door at its end. Benson Culverson opened the first door on the right to reveal a comfortably large room with a pair of bunks mounted to one wall, a couple of lounging chairs and a desk with lamp under a wide but shallow window.

"All the rooms are the same. The larger door at the end is to the bath and storage. Sorry, no separate facilities for the ladies." He mocked regret with a pout and a shrug.

My wife spoke first: "This will do nicely. The kids and I will settle in. Why don't you go along with Mr. Culverson dear? I know you're dying to get to work!"

She was right. What I knew of the situation so far had truly whetted my appetite and fired my imagination. I couldn't wait to see the data they had collected, the research they were doing, or to interview the affected miners.

The younger Culverson exited the module with me close behind and headed for the centrally located, larger module which I took to be the laboratory and base operations center. Though the ground between the modules was well traversed, it maintained a certain springiness that hinted at the thawing mass beneath. Before we could reach the module we had been detected by a swarm of black flies or mosquitos that rose from the moss. Young Culverson broke into a jog to avoid them, and I quickly matched his pace, as my entomological interests at that moment weren't sufficient to overcome the misery they were inflicting.

Once inside the laboratory module and free of our arthrodial assailants, though panting slightly, young Culverson began an immediate tour of the facility. The lab was actually well appointed given its location, though a pall of dust attested to its lack of use.

"As you can tell, we haven't had the best of luck finding help." He smiled sheepishly. "We've got all the best equipment here, and all in working order."

As I looked around the spacious interior, I could see immediately all the necessary devices – microscopes, various mass and infrared spectroscopes, PCR and electrophoresis apparatus, incubation and isolation cabinets, and a hermetically sealed hazmat chamber accessible only via a bubble suit. I was impressed.

"I can't imagine you don't have them knocking down your doors for the chance to work in a lab like this!"

"Well, Dr. Bander, as you know, the demand is high and the supply is low when it comes to the biological sciences right now. So few kids signing up that those who graduate are gobbled up by the big internationals before their graduation caps hit the ground." Benson Culverson's chagrinned look apologized for the smallness of his family's operation. "If you hadn't taken that stroll on the boat's deck on the voyage up, we'd still be looking."

"Meeting your uncle was as fortuitous for me as for Culverson BioTech. Our decision to come north was rather a lark. I had hoped at best to set up a small practice in one of the more remote modular municipalities tending to the needs of the influx of homesteaders. Instead, I find myself employed by a well-respected firm, and supplied with a lab that bests anything I ever had the opportunity to work in. I can tell you this dust will not be untroubled for long!" I hoped I was expressing my enthusiasm without becoming overly rhapsodic.

The young Culverson returned a generous smile. "The pleasure is all ours, Dr. Bander! I assure you!"

Sufficiently reassured, I went right to the business at hand. "So, we have reports of illness of unknown origin; physical injuries do to contact with unknown substances; strange, possibly organic structures – and, oh yes, hallucinations induced by circumstances unknown." I was pleased with my dissertation of the extant facts.

"That's not quite all, doctor. We just got a report this morning not far from where the confused drilling crew was located. Another drilling crew in the area has been electrocuted. Only one man survived, and he's not doing well. Said a lightning bolt came right up out of the drill hole." Benson Culverson's knitted brows indicated how heavily the accumulation of strange occurrences weighed upon him.

"Anyone have any idea how it happened?" This new piece to the puzzle took a considerable swipe at my already burgeoning hypotheses of novel microbes and hallucinogenic gases.

"Well, there are no manmade voltage sources in the area sufficient to have done it – no power lines or underground cables. The drilling rig runs on natural gas, with only a small generator for lights, so it couldn't have been the source. The weather was clear, and weather recordings show no indications of any lightening activity in the area."

With this new puzzle added to the accumulating pieces, I became more anxious than ever to get into the field.

"How quickly can we put together an expedition to the drilling sites?"

"There are two small hovercrafts already fueled and provisioned, under tarps out by the oil tanks. I'll have some of the maintenance crew unwrap them and get them ready. We can leave first thing in the morning, if you care to."

"That would be splendid!" I hoped I hadn't sounded like an overly enthusiastic school-boy, though that's exactly how I felt.

CHAPTER 6

The hovercraft to which young Culverson had referred now sat idling in the well-tracked space between the building where my wife and children were still sleeping and the central collection of storage tanks. It was only 5:00 AM, but being midsummer, the Sun was already well above the horizon to the northeast. A light frost dusted the surrounding tundra, but could be seen retreating steadily under daylight's onslaught. Soon the myriad sucking insects would be sufficiently warmed to begin their daily feasting on all things succulent – plant, animal, or otherwise.

Busy cinching ties, adjusting tarps, and shoving here and there to square the loads were a half-dozen Inuit workers. It was the first I had seen of them, and did not know if they resided in the compound or commuted from a nearby village. Young Culverson was conferring with one of the Inuits, whom I took to be either the foreman of the crew, or perhaps the headman from the village. They were speaking an Inuit dialect, punctuated with the occasional hand sign. As I surveyed the scene it came to me that the strange symbols that I had previously noticed (but not noted) below all visible signs on the premises must in fact be written Inuit.

The hovercraft were smaller versions of the transport that had delivered us to Garry Lake. I was glad to see they had a closed cockpit for the operator and three passengers. Three quarters of their length was a lowered, flat deck, now packed high with containers of equipment, housing, food stuffs, and other essential necessary for setting up a base camp. Two turbo-jets on each side at the stern provide both the hover-thrust and forward propulsion. These were rather outdated models still operated on carbon fuels, but in the end more dependable than some of their modern counterparts, which accounted well in this unforgiving place.

Our course would take us northeast some 80 kilometers to a place called Bromley Lake. It was the location of the test pit where miners had first encountered the corrosive fluids and vapors, and the vein-like, pulsing structures from which they were reported to have issued. I was anxious to get samples at least, and at best to get the chance to examine these structures first hand.

As I approached the hovercraft, young Culverson spied me, and quickly finishing his business with the Inuit, strode my way smiling, and sweeping an arm in the direction of the provisioned hovercraft.

"I think I've got everything covered. Portable lab equipment, bug spray, some fantastic inflatable yurts for shelter, bug spray, enough food and water for two weeks, bug spray…."

At that point he surrendered to his own humor, and laughed heartily. "I guess I'm most own best audience," he gasped between guffaws. Forcefully sobering himself, he took a deep breath: "Sorry, but you've already had a sample of it. It's going to be over 22 degrees today, so the swarms are going to be oppressive! They want our blood!" He smiled sheepishly at his excessive melodrama.

I was all too aware of the increasing insect populations as the climate warmed at these high latitudes. Though the biting insects garnered most of the attention, the warming climate and abundance of flowering plants was proving a boon to the bee population. Whereas human agricultural practices in the lower latitudes had taken a terrible toll on bee populations, the virgin tundra, for thousands of years protected from human exploitation, with its unadulterated flora, proved a windfall for the bees. Surely it would not be long before the opportunity to exploit this emerging resource would begin. Though I love honey, it somehow seemed a shame.

I was not at all empathetic with the rise of the blood-sucking hordes! In fact, one the biological concerns presented by the warming climate and thawing tundra is the release of long dormant microbes that might infect on organism, with the biting flies and mosquitos then serving as vectors of transmission.

Anyway, I was glad we were leaving early, before the swarms could rise from their frigid repose. We would be sheltered most of the day by the hovercraft cockpit, and because the journey would take most of the day in the heavily laden hovercraft, late afternoon chill would already be dampening the enthusiasm (and metabolism) of the sanguinary dipterae.

Young Culverson redeemed me from my musings by touching my shoulder and beckoning toward the nearest hovercraft's open cockpit door. Already the pilots were strapped in and running their preflights, so that the roar of the turbos gave no opportunity for communication, so I entered the cockpit and took the seat directly behind the pilot, the other seats already being taking by two of the Inuit workers. Young Culverson indicated by gesture that he would be riding in the second hovercraft, and with a small, curt salute, headed at a trot in its direction.

As with the journey from Bakers Lake to Garry Lake, the journey to Bromley Lake revealed a seemingly endless expanse of tundra liberally dotted with small lakes and ponds reflecting the unblemished blue of the Arctic sky. Like many, I had assumed the tundra regions to be flat vast plains of moss and lichen. They are in fact anything but flat! The heavily laden hovercraft carried so much momentum that it took considerable and continuous maneuvering by the pilot to keep the craft from overrunning its cushion of air and striking suddenly rising terrain, or plunging bow first into the myriad bodies of water collected in the low places.

Occasionally it was necessary to traverse a particularly steep grade to prevent the craft from oscillating and spilling its cushion of air. Though the ride was not as smooth as I would have preferred, being secure from the great, dark swarms of flies and mosquitoes made any other discomfort seem trivial.

As we traveled we occasionally encountered the grade of a service road constructed by the various mining interests who had and were currently exploring the regions for minerals and other resources. It was often possible to follow these tracks, making the ride smoother. But as it was necessary to seek out suitable ground on the thawing tundra capable of supporting the weight of heavy machinery, most generally the tracks were quite serpentine, imitating in low relief the tortuous trek of a high mountain road. Riding on its slippery ball bearing of air, cut-backs and hair-pin turns are not easily maneuvered in a hovercraft, and if so, only at very slow speeds, so unless such routes fell along our general direction of travel, we kept to our overland course.

We arrived at the southeast shore of Bromley Lake by mid-afternoon. This area had already been the site of much exploration, and a little actual mining. The abandoned pits were easily recognizable by their unnaturally geometric outlines. The deposits in the region being mostly played out, now all that remained were the deserted shells of buildings and the occasional rusting hulk of a machine too worn to be worth salvaging. A few fishing camps still dotted the shore here and there, but with arrival of true summer to the Arctic and the subsequent insect swarms, and also owing to the generally (and in most places severely) depressed economies, sport fishing was practically non-existent. The Inuit, of course, every indomitable and adaptive to this place, still fished the lake and its tributaries.

By the time we crossed the northeast shore of Bromley Lake the late afternoon chill had begun having the hoped for effect on the cold-blooded arthropoda. Though still swarming, their midday frenzy was now reduced to a rather rheumatoidal waltz. Soon they would seek the shelter of tundra vegetation to avoid the frost and await the morrow's warming sun.

CHAPTER 7

Within a couple of kilometers of the lake's shore we encountered the first of the pits excavated by the company contracting with Culverson BioTech. Though the recent occurrences had brought a cessation to work, the pits were still dry, the buildings in good order, and the machinery well-oiled and unrusted. The pilots settled the hovercraft near the complex of buildings. Within an instant I was free of my seatbelt and out the cockpit door. I was anxious to get the opportunity to explore first-hand the phenomena that had put the dampers on this venture.

Most of the workers at the operation had been Inuit, who only reluctantly and out of necessity participated in this great violation of the Mother Earth. The strange occurrences only convinced them that She was striking back at them for the sacrilege. They had quickly and quietly disappeared en masse early the morning following the incident.

As for the workers from the lower latitudes, they continued to make some effort at the company's insistence until the number of injuries and the increasingly toxic environment in the pits made work impossible. Once work ceased, a general unease began to grow. Not knowing the cause or origin of the problems, to a man every employee demanded a transfer and immediate transport to a safe distance. The company had no choice but to abandon the work, at great cost and even greater loss.

Having the facilities of the abandoned camp available to us, it was not necessary on this first leg of our journey to unpack anything more than the lab equipment. The place had been evacuated so quickly that everything remained in place. Sufficient food and other supplies for months, if need be. I did notice that our Inuit friends unpacked their personal gear, which I suspected contained provisions. I appreciated their caution in this place where their world had been violated.

Though the Sun had grown low, night only lasted a scant four hours or so during summer at this latitude, and sunset was a spectacularly protracted affair. With young Culverson's help we quickly located the safety hut, and as quickly secured and donned hazmat suits and respirator helmets. The Inuits kept their distance from us, indicating their reluctance to be involved. We made no attempt to coerce them.

"I won't try to take any samples tonight. I just want to get a look at the place – the general geology and such." I wanted to assure young Culverson that I wasn't going to drag him out into the gathering gloom and then torture him with my obsessive curiosity. I would reign it in and settle for a few moments only.

Young Culverson had supplied me with a report from the mining company, which I had read over during the trip. It indicated that the area of peculiar activity, and thus my interest, lay at the northeast corner of the present excavation. Though only several months old, the dig extended nearly 2 kilometers from the camp at lake's edge to its furthermost northeast extension. Once suited up and making our way towards the pit, young Culverson indicated to me by a touch and a directed nod of his now hermetically helmeted head what appeared to be two one-man hoverods. Stepping onto the platform of the nearest one, he gripped its activator/rudder and the device immediately came to life. Much like the antique Segways I'd ridden as a boy, the devices sensed body location for steerage and speed. Young Culverson had obviously had considerable experience with such devices, and deftly levitated, came about, and headed for the far wall of the excavation. A little more cautiously, I stepped onto my device, and after a moment's hesitation, gripped the activator/rudder. Like so many things – once mastered; never forgotten – I found I had little trouble navigating the hoverod, and was soon following closely behind young Culverson.

I slowed as I approached the pit's far wall. It was terraced into three levels, the lowest being the richest ore deposit. The second and upper most terraces were points of overburden removal. The wall of the first terrace was a profile of the tundral soil and regolith that overlay the bedrock. According to the report I had read, the first of the vein like structures were encountered in removing the tundral overburden. No particularly adverse effects on humans were noted, except that owing to the extremely tough and fibrous nature of the stuff, it continually clogged the gears and tracks of the earth moving equipment, or got wrapped around an axle or a drive shaft, bring the equipment to a complete halt.

The report also indicated that similar structures were encounter in crevices and voids in the bedrock at the lowest level. It was here that the caustic and toxic emissions were encountered. I used the hazmat suits communicator to query young Culverson.

"So, no reports of caustic fluids or noxious fumes at this level?"

He nodded his assurance.

"Well, let's take a look down there." I pointed my chin to the edge of the precipice that constituted the wall of the lower pit. "We'll have to be careful. Watch your suit's reading carefully. Don't get too close to any of the machinery. A rip or tear in a suit could be disastrous. We'd have to purge and evacuate immediately."

Young Culverson listen politely to my admonitions, though they were certainly unnecessary. In fact, they were more intended as a verbal reminder to myself of the possible dangers.

Immediately upon initiating our descent, alarms on the suit sensors began to chime, and their lights to flash. Looking at the array of indicators located along the top of the left-forearm of the suit's sleeve, I quickly activated the readout screen. The indications were toxic and caustics gases, the readout quickly passing these identities: hydrogen cyanide 1000 ppm; cyanogen chloride 6000 ppm, hydrogen chloride 1100 ppm. The device continued to list all detected substances, but I had seen enough. All the values given were toxic; fatal. No unprotected human could survive more than a few agonizing minutes in that environment. But men had escaped, so obviously the situation had gotten much worse, indicating that the source or sources of these substances were still active.

I turned to young Culverson and saw that he too was closely examining his readouts. He turned to me, and through the visor of his hazmat helmet I could see the puzzled expression on his face.

"Not a very friendly place. I don't think our present equipment is up to the task. Let's head back. Lights fading. We need to sit down and create a plan of attack."

Young Culverson did not respond, except for the expression of relief that crossed his countenance. Silently, then, with only the whir of the hoverods, we made our course toward the mining camp. The Sun was now low enough to reveal a brilliant borealis dancing and flaming in the northern sky, its curtain of colors reflected in the myriad mirrors of tundral pools.

Once back at the camp, safely decontaminated, denuded, and debrided in the quarantine module, we donned the camp's traditional overall garb and headed for the already lighted module we hoped would be the camp cafeteria. As we approached, the scent of coffee and roasting meat certified our speculation.

Young Culverson and I had exchanged few words since our return from the pit, only the necessary instructions and courtesies exchanged during our decontamination. But theories had been percolating in both our minds the entire time, and now reached the point of eruption. I was the first to speak.

"I don't understand all the cyanide at that depth? It can be produced by certain types of combustion, and I guess perhaps pockets could have formed in the rock. But mostly it's an organically generated substance. But what type of organism could exist in sufficient number to produce those quantities? I mean, I know there are some extremophile bacteria and archaea found deep in rock formations, but surely not in sufficient quantities or with sufficient capacity to produce that many and that volume of cyanide compounds."

Young Culverson, with degrees in biology and bioengineering had speculations of his own: "Perhaps it's some new strain of bacteria or fungi; something never seen before. I mean, it's the reason we're here, to see if the thaw uncovers something buried for millennia. Lots of organisms utilize cyanic compounds as defense. Maybe something's been uncovered that's just trying to defend itself?"

My own thoughts were running parallel to young Culverson's. We stopped just in front of the galley module's door and faced each other. Our brows furrowed as deeply as a farmer's fields, we exchanged very penetrating, inquisitive glances.

I offered some relief from our consternation: "Let's see what's cooking. Sometimes a hot cup of coffee and a little nourishment help clear the mind." Young Culverson smiled his agreement, and we abandoned the luminiferous Arctic eve for the well-lit and savory fragrance of the mess hall.

The sudden change in lighting caused a mild squint, but soon enough the room came into focus. As with industrial mess halls everywhere, this one contained a shiny, stainless steel food line along one wall, the rest of the space taken up the by geometrically precise placement of dining tables with attached seating. The hall was obviously meant to serve hundreds at a time; our small gathering of eight barely intruded on its vast interior.

The Inuit I took earlier to be a head-man rose from his lone place at a table. The hoverod pilots and other workers, all Inuits, congregated at a table some distance away, turned their attention to us upon seeing the man rise. It reinforced my sense of the man's authority. He was obviously the man in charge of this BioTech crew; his dignity and bearing, and the attention paid him by the others indicated he was much more.

He approached us with that grin characteristic of his people. It was both a warm greeting, and a habit born of adaptation to a snow-covered world beneath the long Arctic summer sun. Of course, given the present climactic conditions, the latter could be discounted.

He gestured toward the food line. "Got some *Tuktu*, ..er caribou, roasted; got some boiled *Masru* ..er roots; got some pudding, *Ittukpalak* – very delicious! Got some hot coffee!!" He was well pleased to announce such an abundant menu. The workforce at the Bromley Lake pit had been 90% Inuit, so I was not too surprised by the food choices. I had actually bothered to study the Inuit language a little on the boat ride up. I was not familiar with the pudding: *Ittukpalak*, however. I turned a questioning face to young Culverson.

"Made from fish eggs and berries." He raised his eyebrows in anticipation of my reaction. He smiled at my rather tentative acceptance of such a proposition, and followed quickly: "Really quite delicious!"

The head-man led us to the food line, and by gesture indicated where to find the necessary eating utensils. I engaged him with a small query as we filled out plates.

"I understand your men will not help us in the pit?" Young Culverson had warned me back at

Garry Lake that we could not count on help from the Inuit. It was bad enough that they were employed to strip the Mother Earth. They now believed that She had reacted to the injury.

The Inuit head-man thought a moment, and then facing me squarely said: "The Inuit know this place, it is near to the land of *Sinnektomanerk*, the place of dreams!"

"The place of dreams?' I looked to young Culverson, who only shrugged. The head-man continued.

"In the world there are places where the *arnirniq*, ...the spirits... speak. We approach such a place. It is the home of *Ignirtoq*, whose wisdom and knowledge shine too brightly for a man's mind. Men are blinded by it!"

I listened intently to the head-man's narration. Considering that much of aboriginal myth and legend are merely attempts by non-scientific men to explain natural phenomena, I questioned the old man:

"These places...are they guarded by other spirits?" Out of the corner of my eye I noted the approving nod of young Culverson to this line of questioning.

"Yes. The *Tarnat!* They can be good or evil. They can bring forth the killing mist; or summon the lightening!"

It was clear that the head-man was aligning his cultural pantheon with recent events. Yet, was he also eluding to previous events known to his people that were similar? I didn't want to challenge his argument for fear of discouraging his openness. I let the conversation end for the time being with a perfunctory: "Very interesting. Very interesting indeed!"

We had filled our plates during the dialogue, and nodding acquiescence, allowed the head-man to lead us to his table. We ate in silence. I saw that the Inuit men at the far table were engaged in animated discourse. Surely they were speculating on what had passed between their elder and the interloping white men, the *kablunak*. When we had finished our meal, and were drinking coffee, the headman spoke:

"It is only for the *angakkuq*, the shamasal, to travel to the place of dreams." The headman paused, seeming to consult the dark liquid surface of his coffee as if it were an oracle. "I will go into the pit with you tomorrow. I will travel with you to the place where lightening comes from the Earth. I will go with you to the place of dreams."

He fell silent again, and sipped his coffee. My supposition as to the source of the headman's authority became certain. Though I was strongly inclined to question him further, his demeanor and posture indicated our conversation was over. I offered only a very respectful: "Thank you." The headman nodded, and putting down his cup and looking at no one, rose from his place at the table, and with great poise strode to the door and out into the summer Arctic's night.

CHAPTER 8

The next morning, over coffee and a scramble of reconstituted eggs and mystery meat, young Culverson and I discussed our plans for the day. We had already sent a couple of the workers to retrieve three of the more substantial environmental suits still packed onto one of the hoverods. The rather flimsy suits in the camp's hazmat wardrobe were not sufficient for spending the time needed in the pit collecting samples and data.

We had hoped to find the headman breakfasting, but were informed he had already been and gone, but left a note that he would return by 8:00 AM. It was only 7:30, so young Culverson and I took our time over our victuals, and both having brought our satellite netpads, were busy taking notes, researching the particulars of the facts known to date, and creating an itinerary for the day.

Actually, young Culverson and I were stretching the bounds of our expertise in pursuing this investigation. Everything thus far seemed to indicate a much greater correlation with geology than biology. On its face, the pit revealed the geologic structure or the site. The "lightening" from the drill hole scenario certainly suggested some sort of geomagnetic phenomenon. And the fact that the "place of dreams" seemed to have a precise geologic location implied some sort of an anomaly relating to the geology of the place rather than a portal to the world of spirits. Any professional deficiencies accounted, our enthusiasm was not daunted.

"First and foremost I want to try and get a sample of the *vein* material. I mean, it could be some sort of spontaneously forming polymer, or more likely a novel type of bacterial colony – a chemotroph feeding on natural chemical reactions in the different layers of strata and gluing itself together into fibrous tubules." I was staring at a spoonful of the gelatinous chemical concoction sitting atop my fork while talking, and as a point of emphasis proffered it to young Culverson. Young Culverson smiled in understanding.

"Yes, there's probably going to be some really mundane explanation for what has occurred here." He signaled disappointment at his own suggestion. He, like me, was hoping that what we found would be something extraordinary.

A sudden flash of light indicated the opening of mess hall's door. Turning to look, we saw the silhouette of the headman approaching us. He came to within a few paces and stopped, still backlit by the light from the open door.

"We should begin. Each moment we tarry brings greater apprehension to the crew." He abruptly turned and moved toward the door. His manner demanded – better yet, commanded – our obedience. We grabbed the remnants of our morning's fare and followed him, hastily depositing the last of the cryptic cuisine in trash bins near the door.

We did not catch up with the headman until we reached the hazmat module, where the workers had already unpacked and laid out our environmental suits. These suits, unlike the camp's equipment, were designed for long-term immersion in hostile environments. They were hermetically sealed from head to toe, the joints at the wrists and helmet not unlike those used in astronautical gear. The suits contained oxygen supplies and carbon dioxide scrubbers in a hard shell pack attached at the back. Solar/battery driven air-conditioning, both heating and cooling, were also housed there. The suit itself was constructed of a laminated material that was chemically resistant, and provided both thermal and radiation shielding. A mesh of tungsten alloy embedded in the laminate gave protection against explosions and projectiles. A pressure sensitive exoskeletal system of hydraulics built into the fabric provided a small amount of assistance when loads exceeded human muscular capacity. Two curved cylinders containing electrolytic fluids and a carbohydrate mash attached at the nape of the helmet, providing liquids and energy through tubes passing through the visor. Atop each helmet was a transceiver capable of receiving and broadcasting up to 5 kilometers. Urine could be recycled if necessary; a diaper was the only accommodation for other circumstances.

No one spoke unnecessarily during the suit-up. Though I was sure the headman had never quite experienced such elaborate attire, he seemed quite at ease during the process, with no reluctance to accept direction from myself or young Culverson. Once suited-up, I indicated to the others to test communications by tapping at the transceiver on my helmet. Voice activated, we had only to mutter a simple syllable.

"I'm here." Culverson kept it simple.

"Here as well," I replied.

"All this magic! Yet, you are troubled to contemplate the Spirit." The headman turned abruptly to the door, having wanted no reply. We followed him silently into the bright Arctic day. Workers had already prepared the hoverods, loading them with the equipment we would need to collect our samples. We each stepped onto our machines. With an unexpected grace and expertise, the headman rounded-to on his hoverod and sped off in the direction of the pit.

I had the day's itinerary firmly fixed in my mind. First and foremost, I wanted to find a sample of a *vein*, and hopefully whatever it contained. I pinned the hoverod against the face of the excavation just where the soils and regolith met the bedrock. Directly I located a shriveled, tubular body protruding slightly from the soil/regolith boundary. The suit's gloves being far too clumsy for fine maneuvering, I retrieved a large set of pick-ups from the equipment pack, and grasping as much of the thing as I could, I began to tug. The material stretched considerably, revealing that it continued deep into the face of the soil. The newly exposed part was not yet shriveled and was quite elastic. I decided to cut-off as large a sample as possible, which, when accomplished, the soil bound part snapped back like a rubber band, into the soil and out of sight. Immediately, a small amount of clear liquid spewed forth from the small hole remained. As quickly as possible I grabbed a small sample bottle to catch a few drops of the unknown substance. It had no more viscosity than water, nor any apparent smell, as the particulate sensors on the suit's sleeves and gloves gave no indication. Satisfied that I had acquire sufficient material from this location, I turned to check on the whereabouts of my companions.

Like myself, young Culverson had pinned his hoverod to the excavation's face and was busy probing and scraping for samples. The headman, however, hovered some distance off the face, standing silently, with his arms extended and his face turned skyward. He appeared to be engaging in a spiritual union with some unseen force; perhaps a prayer of forgiveness for those who continued to injure the Mother Earth.

"I've got enough here, think I'll go on down the bottom." Young Culverson looked my way and nodded.

"I'll be along shortly. Still looking here."

The headman neither acknowledged my communication, nor changed his stance.

Quickly descending to the bottom of the pit, I again pinned the hoverod against the excavation's face. This time I selected a spot obviously creviced, with evidence of the seepage of some sort of fluid. I was not disappointed by my choice. For two adjacent crevices, separated by no more ten centimeters, I again found shriveled remnants of the tubular structures. This time however, the fluids issuing forth set off sensors on the suit's sleeves. A slightly viscous, slightly colored liquid issuing from the left most crevice indicated the presence of hydrocyanic and hydrochloric acids. I collected a sample. The fluid issuing from the right crevice indicated it was basic in nature from the pH sensor. Though the sensors were not specific enough to determine absolute identity, they indicated the presence of metal chlorides and metal cyanides. Again I gathered samples. I also repeated the earlier process of extracting a sample of the tubular material.

Having gathered sufficient samples, I was eager to return to the lab to begin analysis. Young Culverson had not joined me in the lower pit, so I radioed my result.

"I've got more than enough stuff here to work with for now. How about we head back to camp." I hoped young Culverson wouldn't object at not having had the opportunity to explore the lower pit.

"Sound's fine to me. Got a good sample of some kind of tubular tissue, I think. I ran a check on the fluid contents with the small mass spectrometer. Looks like the stuff is just water, but not JUST water – it's about 80% pure deuterium oxide – heavy water!" His pronouncement elicited the same excitement in me that his voice expressed.

Rising to ground level just as young Culverson disengaged from the excavation face, I noted that the headman had already turned his hoverod in the direction of camp and was making way apace. Without a word, he proceeded us there. By the time we arrived, he was already unsuiting. Young Culverson and I had quarantine protocols to follow before unsuiting, so the headman was gone long before we made it to the decontamination room to unsuit. I hoped our activities on that day had not earned his disapproval, or proved a sacrilege. More importantly, I hoped he would still accompany us further – to the place of dreams.

CHAPTER 9

"**D**efinitely organic in origin. I can see the cell structure under low magnification!" The excitement in young Culverson's voice was electric! "I'll try some staining to see if I can bring up some internal structures."

While young Culverson worked on the now confirmed tissue samples, I had already begun a search for organic molecules, both in the hard samples, and in the fluids. I began by sonically lysing a small bit of a tissue sample; then using surfactant to remove the lipids. Protease and then RNase were added to catalyze proteins and RNA into their soluble constituents. Finally, ethanol precipitation was used to coagulate the DNA. The sample was then centrifuged. To my consternation no DNA pellet formed! I ran several more samples, but always with the same result – no DNA!

Perplexed by my results, I approached young Culverson, who seemed equally confounded by his results.

"How's the staining going?"

"It's not! I tried several times, but can't find any defined internal structure. Whatever it is, it's gotta be very primitive!"

"Well, that's what we've come looking for. I guess we shouldn't be surprised. What is surprising is that I'm not finding any DNA. How could these cells have replicated themselves, much less combined into a structure, without DNA?"

My question hit a chord somewhere in young Culverson's psyche. He turned inward for a moment, then burst forth with a rapid accounting of his findings.

"Ya' know, I did a little brushing up on my protobiology before coming north, particularly pithoviruses, which have been found in similar environments. We could be looking at something here that is more primitive than bacteria! And if you accept that RNA preceded DNA, well then – eureka!"

I had followed young Culverson's argument well enough, though I hadn't done any brushing up. It made sense.

"So, I need to see if I can extract RNA?"

"I think so. You know it's long been argued that the first true life on the planet probably developed in the crevices of hot rocks. Maybe we've found the proof!" Young Culverson seem pleased with his appraisal.

"I'll give it a shot. But RNA is so damned sensitive that it's hard to sequester. Always a dozen different things working to break it down." Determined, but not overly hopeful, I prepared to return to the hunt. But with these developments, I was more than interested in the make-up of the fluids we had gathered. "Why don't you focus on the fluid samples. See if you're really seeing that concentration of heavy water. And the suit sensors only indicate the general nature of the stuff from the bottom of the pit. See if you can narrow it down." With a plan in place, we returned to our respective areas and dug-in.

So many hypotheses now crowded my thoughts it was difficult to focus on the RNA extraction. Something so primitive as to contain only RNA – we were possibly talking LUCA: *the last universal common ancestor!* But that still didn't jive with the structure. Bacteria grow in colonies, of course. But for a primitive organism to colonize into useful structures – but then there are jelly fish! And fungi! But they all contain DNA. I shook my head to dislodge the speculating, and focused on extraction of RNA. And after the first attempt, there it was! Not wanting to shout it out for fear of startling young Culverson during some delicate procedure, I crossed the lab in great strides to deliver the news.

Young Culverson turned as I approached, obviously cued by the sound of my footsteps. As I was about to speak, I saw on his face an expression that told me he had something perhaps as important to tell me as I supposed my findings were. He began to speak immediately.

"A couple of things….First, I did find one interesting structure in the cells – what appears to be plasmodesmata!"

Plasmodesmata are tiny holes in the walls between some plant cells that permit molecules to pass directly from one cell to the next. But these were obviously not plant cells. It seemed the confusion was multiplying itself. My offering suddenly seemed anticlimactic.

"Well, I found the RNA. It's extremely varied, coding for a lot of different proteins. How it manages to grow a *vein*, though…..I don't know. It seems to fall into the LUCA category. There are only the four RNA nucleotides: adenine, guanine, cytosine and uracil. But how to account for the diversity?" I saw that young Culverson was intently assaying my results.

"What about ATP?" Culverson's question was a real head slapper.

"Of course – ATP. It'll just take a moment to check. A little ultraviolet light…." I was half-way across the lab before I finished the sentence.

All organisms need a way to store and transmit the energy needed for life processes. The molecule adenosine triphosphate, ATP, is the molecule all life on earth uses for this purpose. No sooner than I illuminated a sample with ultraviolet light, the telltale glow of light reflected from ATP appeared. Another question answered; a dozen more presented. Young Culverson had found no apparent structures within the tissue cells, so what was the origin of the ATP? Young Culverson approached my work station with head nodding as he too saw the glow.

"There's got to be more to this thing. Something we're not seeing yet. We've got tissued structures whose obvious purpose is the transport and delivery of fluids – but transported to where?"

Young Culverson's question was not lost on me. We needed to determine the relationship, if any, between what we had found in the pit, and the electrical phenomenon that had been encountered kilometers to the northeast. But first we needed to more closely examine the fluids found.

"You're certain that the fluid from the upper cut was predominately heavy water?"

"Absolutely." Young Culverson's confidence was unshaken by my query.

"Well, we need to take a closer look at the fluids from the lower pit. Anything you noticed right off the bat?"

Young Culverson answered immediately: "Yes, certain of the *veins* obviously deliver the solvents, while others return solutions to some unknown place. Though we don't see it now – only seepage – according to the miners' reports, when they first severed the veins they seemed to have a pulse. So we can work from the angle that somewhere there's a pump moving this stuff – maybe some kind of a primitive heart, but on a large scale – a circulatory system for some sort of organism…?" Young Culverson's voiced pitched upwards and faded as new possibilities presented themselves.

"Have you run any tests on the solutions?"

"Yes, the sensors were right about the hydrochloric acid and nitric acids, and the metal cyanides. They seem to be associated with the delivery side of system. The return solutions seem primarily made up of palladium chlorides and platinum and palladium cyanide complexes." Young Culverson paused a moment as possibilities ebbed and flowed in his analytical machinery. Then, with a curiously ominous tone to his voice, he pronounced quite assuredly: "It seems men aren't the only ones mining here!"

I, of course, had been piecing the puzzle together as rapidly as he. But with all the disparate pieces of information, it was hard to imagine what we were dealing with. The seemingly purposeful extraction of minerals by structures so primitive in their make-up that they defied classification just didn't make sense. Surely we were only glimpsing the peripheral feeding organs of something much larger. But what? What feeds on heavy water and palladium? It all seemed so absurd my thoughts retreated to the consideration of the electrical discharge to the northeast. I shared my speculation with young Culverson.

"This may sound like a bit of stretch, but could there be a link between what we've found here and the electrocution of the drillers up to the northeast? I'm probably grabbing at straws, but when you're looking for needle in a haystack it's to be expected I guess." The humor was pretty lame and young Culverson had only acknowledged it with a rather anemic smile. Yet, he agreed.

"I think you're right. We got a bunch of puzzle pieces here that don't seem to make sense. We should widen our search. I'll talk to the foreman and have the crew ready us for an expedition to the drilling site."

Young Culverson and I tidied up our work areas, and without a word departed the labs for the mess hall. The rest of the crew were already there – the pilots and workers at their usual table, the headman alone at his. We went straight to the food line, and the headman not giving us so much as glance, we took a table somewhat removed from the rest. We ate silently, our minds such a whir that meaningful conversation was not possible. When I had finished, I rose and bid young Culverson a distracted "See you in the morning." Just as I exited I noticed young Culverson get up and walk toward the headman. At this point I was not interested in their business, and headed for my sleeping quarters.

The warp and weave of an exceptional Borealis played through and reflected off the slats of the jalousie shutters on the module's windows. The dancing colors soon lulled me into a semi-conscious state, the cogitating part of my mind running full bore as the dreamy sub-conscious, augmented my thoughts with great luminescent, throbbing jellyfish and multicolored, glowing mushrooms the size of houses. I had the strangest sensation of falling – falling down a rabbit hole.... Yet, I felt perfectly calm; the phantasms dancing before me, though curious, did not seem abnormal. In fact, I had felt absolutely normal in a most uncommon way. The rational part of my mind had accepted as plausible the most irrational of propositions, as jellyfish and mushrooms alike engaged me in all manner of philosophical and scientific discourse.

CHAPTER 10

My somnambulistic adventures ended abruptly as a shaft of morning sunlight fell across my face. As I ascended from the depths, I kept telling myself: "I must remember…!" Of course, upon attaining a fully wakeful state, all the night's apparitions evaporated like a morning's mist. For a moment or two I tried to retrieve them, but to no avail. I was left with the feeling of something lost, but put it aside and dressed and prepared for the day's tasks.

Exiting my quarters into the already brilliant morning sun, I quickly noted the preparations for our excursion underway. The Inuit workers, under the direction of the headman, were busy reloading the lab equipment onto two of the hovercraft; the remaining hovercraft would remain as a precaution at the mining site. In addition to lab equipment and supplies, two hoverods were being lashed astern, one to each of the hovercraft. Also, several crates clearly marked as property of the mining site were being loaded. I was curious, but would wait to inquire, as stimulation of the vagus nerve in the region of my stomach induced a rather urgent sense of hunger.

Young Culverson was already in the mess hall when I arrived. He hailed me, and with a sweep of his arm in the direction of the food line indicated I should avail myself of some sustenance before joining him. He began the conversation as I approached with a plate full of the ubiquitous morning scramble.

"We'll be ready to go as soon as we've eaten. They're just finishing the loading now." The last syllable was immediately followed by a fork full of the gelatinous scramble.

"I see they're loading some of the camp's equipment as well…" I too wasted no time between gabbling and gobbling. I had become quite fond of the conglomerate cuisine.

"Yes! The foreman thought it best to take some tools and spare parts for the drilling rig. He thinks it's likely to have suffered from the electrical discharge. We'll want to retrieve the core if possible, to see if there's anything down there to explain the discharge."

I nodded agreement, and returned to my epicurean efforts, swallowing large bites of the scramble followed by gulps of the hot, dark brew that served as coffee.

Just as we finished and rose to leave, young Culverson offered up this additional information:

"Of course, you know that it'll only be you, me, and the foreman going? The others won't go…" He looked to see if I was surprised by the revelation. I was not. I had gathered from the headman's reticence in past days that we were close to treading on Inuit tradition.

"Do you think we'll be able to get the rig running?" My mechanical skills were somewhat lacking; I didn't know if young Culverson had any.

"The foreman's got a degree in engineering. I think he'll be able to handle it. By the way, his name is Anuniaq – I won't even attempt his shaman name! He has ask that we call him Anun. He says he will watch over us in the coming days." Young Culverson squinted a little as he made these pronouncements, checking to see that I understood their full implications. I nodded affirmatively.

It was about 60 kilometers from the mining site at Bromley Lake to the drill site where the crew had been electrocuted. Anun took the lead in one hovercraft; I rode with young Culverson who piloted the second – not expertly, but adequately. The craft were so heavily ladened and top heavy, the going was slow. With only the three of us, capsizing one of the craft would have proved disastrous. So, with Anun in the lead, we made our way cautiously across the open tundra, avoiding steep inclines and declines and sharp turns. As a result, our course was circuitous, and our progress slow.

I was glad we had Anun to navigate our course. At such high latitudes, compass dip and anomaly, the nearly circumferential transit of the sun, and all manner of electrical disturbances to affect satellite signals made high-tech navigation nearly impossible. It took the eye and innate senses of a native to safely find one's way across the tundra.

The radios were silent as we made our serpentine course across what had for so long seemed a vast Arctic wasteland to those of my ilk. My brief encounter with the men of this region to date – their tenacity; their ingenuity; their culture – had quickly dispelled my former notions. The farther into the wilderness I wandered, the less wilderness I found. It seemed man was the master everywhere, after all.

After what seemed an interminable time, the radios crackling brought me from my reveries. Anun's voice, his English heavily flavored with a seasoning of his native tongue, announced our arrival.

"Rig's just ahead. Settin' on the edge of water. Watch ya' don't set down on somethin' too soft."

Young Culverson eased our hovercraft from behind Anun's for a better view. I could see the small derrick of the coring rig across a considerable expanse of water mirroring blue, cloudless sky. The rig was set up in a low area, so it would be necessary to make certain we found firm footing for landing. It would not take much subsidence of the thawing tundra for the top-heavy hovercraft to take a tumble.

The drilling rig sat upon a triangular, self-leveling pontoon that allowed it to be set on land or water. The pontoon served not only as floatation, but as living quarters, core shed, and storage as well. Though initially airlifted to a general location, thrusters at its three vertices allowed it to be moved the small distances required to create a core-sample grid. The survivor had been doing maintenance work on one of thrusters when the discharge occurred, and was thrown clear of the rig. The others had been engaged in drilling, and were on the derrick, or at the core hole when the discharge occurred. According to the survivor, after landing flat on his back on a soggy patch of tundra, though nearly immobilized by the shock, he was facing the rig sufficiently to see the several second discharge dance about in great electrical arcs from the core hole to various targets on the pontoon, some of which were his unfortunate comrades.

The open areas atop the pontoon were not sufficient to accommodate objects the size or our hovercraft, so young Culverson hovered near the rig while Anun scouted a landing area. About a hundred meters just east of the rig a small rise gave promise, and after circling its perimeter, and landing gently, Anun radioed his appraisal.

"Look's like it will do. Wait a bit, see if it settles any." After a moments silence: "All right, then. Come on over. Seems okay. Set down close to me as you can."

I remained silent during young Culverson's maneuvers. The intense bite he inflicted on his lower lip indicated he was too preoccupied for conversation. Any lack of skill on his part as a pilot was overcome by his intensity. He set our hovercraft down parallel and within a meter of Anun's, with scarcely a glitch, save the sweat pouring down his face and dripping onto the console. Once aground, he released his white-knuckled grip on the control yoke, and sitting back, exhaled dramatically.

"Well, that wasn't so bad." The tone of his voice was mildly demonstrative, but audibly plaintive. He turned a gave me a nervous smile.

"Any landing you walk away from is a good landing!" I rejoined, parroting a quip I had often overheard among aviation types engaged in mutual inebriation.

Without further exchange we exited the hovercraft's cockpit. Anun was already busy unlashing the hoverod at the stern of his craft. Young Culverson nodded toward ours: "Don't know if I can pilot one of those with two aboard. Why don't you follow Anun over and have a look while I unpack some gear? Maybe I ought to inflate a couple of the yurts. Probably be better to plan on staying over here tonight, until we figure out what's going on." I nodded an agreement, and headed to the stern to unlash the second hoverod.

Anun was already unlashed, with his hoverod idling. He waited patiently as I freed mine and prepared it for flight. As quickly as I had it fired up, Anun mounted his and headed for the rig. I followed as quickly and gracefully as I could. Once near the rig, Anun gunned his thrusters, bringing the hoverod to the height of the rig's pontoon deck. His voice activated transmission brought my headset to life. "You, wait there a bit. I'll land first. See if it's safe. No use both takin' a chance", said as matter-of-factly as if he were reciting instructions from a manual.

I watched as he maneuvered slowly but precisely into one of the small open areas on the pontoon's deck. With generators, hydraulic pumps, stacks of drill rod, and barrels covering most of the available space, it took a rather precise maneuver to place the hoverod. He hovered for a moment a meter or so above an open space before committing to a landing, no doubt hoping to determine whether another electrical discharge awaited. Finally letting the craft ease on to the deck with no consequence, he quickly killed its thrusters, and radioed: "Seems okay. Come on up. Gonna be tight. Don't want to wreck nothin', so be careful."

Successfully, though in no way as gracefully as Anun, I managed to put my hoverod on the pontoon's deck. By the time I had shut down the thrusters, Anun was already inspecting the equipment, beginning with the generator, the rig's heart. I could see the charred and metal splattered points where the electrical arcs from the discharge had grounded. Ominously, one such point held the unmistakable outline of a man's shoes.

Anun's voice crackled in my headset: "Looks like the diodes in the regulator are fried. Got some spares. I'll get it workin', then we can see 'bout the motors. Don't seem to be no charges built up on anythin'. Why don't you check below, see what ya' can find."

I waved an okay to the headman, and headed for the ladder to the interior of the pontoon. I switched on the headlamp imbedded in my helmet and descended the ladder cautiously. I was immediately greeted by the unpleasant odor of putrefaction. Since all the occupants of the rig had been accounted for, I concluded it must be something in the food stores. The refrigeration has been inoperative for several days now, and though the weather was cool, any fresh meats or vegetables would have begun to decay.

Sweeping the beam of my headlamp around, I saw that a central corridor ran from the open public space at the bottom of the ladder. All along the corridor were hatches to what I supposed to be individual crew cabins. Here and there charring around fixtures and along pipes indicated the discharge had arced through the interior of the pontoon as well. Other than that, there seemed nothing worth investigating. Though I had developed a tolerance for the odors of putrefaction during my tenure as a medical doctor, I preferred to evacuate the space as soon as possible. Only breathing in gulps, I hastened up the ladder, anxious to breathe some fresh air.

Just as I obtained the deck, the grind and whine of the generator's starter motor indicated Anun had made his repairs. The engine belched a couple of clouds of black smoke, then caught and quickly ran up to operational rpms. Anun turned immediately to the distribution panel, and open all but the lighting circuits. Engaging the main buss, most of the lights on the pontoon and derrick flashed on. Those that didn't had probably been damaged by the discharge. A few more immediately extinguished with a pop! As Anun turned his attentions to the various motors that operated the pumps and winches, I turned my attention to the bore-hole at the base of the derrick.

There could be little doubt that the discharge originated from the bore. The drill rod was charred and metal had splattered from the hot spots where the charge had exited. I was anxious to get the core sample raised, to see if it could give us information as to the cause of the discharge.

CHAPTER 11

By late afternoon the headman had the necessary pumps and wenches running. Young Culverson had made camp, so I returned on the hoverod to gather him and some sample bottles. I was glad for the yurts, as the condition below decks at the rig were not conducive to habitation. Not trusting my pilotage with two aboard, I surrendered command of the hoverod to young Culverson. His difficulty in maneuvering the craft under the additional load affirmed my choice – I certainly would have crashed!

Once at the rig, we wasted no time working on raising the core sample. Anun had checked the derrick and drill rod in the bore for any residual charges or unusual electric activity. He detected a weak, pulsing DC voltage, without apparent cause. But at only a few millivolts, and no measurable current, it posed no threat of discharge. We decided to proceed, so with the wench engaged, we began extracting the three meter sections of drill rod. Nine three meter core samples lay in trays adjacent to the bore hole, leading us to conclude that the sample we would be retrieving was from a depth of about 30 meters.

The core bit was a hollow three-meter tube of harden steel with a toothed cut edge at its lower end. As the cutting edge deepened the bore, a cylindrical core sample was captured in the hollow of the tube. Such core samples taken from a grid of core holes allowed one to create a profile of the underlying geology. We were anxious to see the core sample in process when the discharge occurred.

Neither young Culverson nor myself had any rough necking experience, but once again the headman proved proficient. We were assigned to operate the wench and power tongs levers, at the headman's direction, of course, and to lend a little muscle when it came to swinging the loose drill rod onto one of the storage racks. After several hours of intense labor, and a lowering Arctic summer sun, the attachment end of the core drill came into site. We quickly and carefully extracted it from the bore hole, and laid it onto an empty sample cradle. Using a hydraulic plunger we gently pushed the sample from the bit, the tube sliding back to allow the sample to ease into the cradle.

A quick example of the core indicated nothing extraordinary, but upon examining the bit, we found material clinging to the cutting teeth, and filling the spiral debris channels which fed the tailings up the outside of the sample tube. In collecting this material, I was immediately struck by its seemingly organic nature. Young Culverson, working at my side, also noted the nature of the material, and immediately commented.

" Damn! That looks a lot like the stuff we recovered from the pit!"

I was as excited as he, but my mental frenzy paralyzed any external expression. I do not now know if I had expected a connection between the finds at the pit and what would be found at the drill site, or if I had secretly wished there would be such a connection. Whichever the case, the reality sent me reeling. Young Culverson remained quietly at my side, obviously appreciating the impact the revelation had upon me. Soon, I was sufficiently composed to respond:

"Yes! At least the stuff in the grooves. But the tissue caught in the teeth seems a bit different." I was cautious with this remark, although young Culverson immediately nodded his agreement. "It appears as though only the cutting head came in contact with whatever it is – there's no sign of tissue in the core sample. Whatever set of the discharge must have been right on the surface of this thing." Again young Culverson nodded agreement.

All the while young Cuvlerson and I had been making our observations, the headman Anun had been standing silently behind us. I turned, hoping maybe to get his opinion, but as soon as I turned, he turned in the direction of his hoverod. Over his shoulder he said: "Best get your stuff together. Sun's gettin' low. Need to get back to camp 'fore it's too dark." He continued to his hoverod, and gathering up a few loose tools into his boxes and securing them, fired up its thrusters, lifted off, and headed in the direction of camp. I turned back to young Culverson.

"Were you able to get the lab yurt set up?"

"Yes. Got all the equipment inside, but not uncrated."

"Let's get back then. I'm anxious to look at this stuff under a microscope!"

We worked silently collecting and sealing our samples. We placed them in storage boxes on the hoverod, and with young Culverson now again in control, we departed the rig. The headman had left the generator running and the lights on, so that most of our journey back to camp was well illuminated. By the time we arrived, Anun had already opened the mess crate, fired up the cook stove, and was preparing a muddy brown stew of uncertain make-up, though with a delightful, meaty aroma. Young Culverson and I headed immediately in the inflated laboratory yurt. We set up tables and uncrated microscopes, centrifuges, electrophoresis equipment, a small mass spectrometer, and a combination spectrophotometer/gas chromatograph. The accuracy of these compact instruments would not be sufficient to be definitive, but they would certainly suffice to give us an idea of the general make-up of our samples.

We had just finished getting things set-up, in anticipation of examining our samples when the headman threw open the yurt's door flap. "Come eat. Ain't polite to keep a man waitin' for his supper. Getting' late. Time tomorrow for that stuff." He spoke matter-of-factly, yet with an air of authority not to be ignored. Like obedient sons to a stern father, we dusted our hands from our work, and followed him silently outside.

The evening sun skipped along the horizon to the northwest, its light now sufficiently mellowed to permit a blaze of borealis to dominate the northeastern sky. Soon the sun would dip just below the horizon enough for the brighter stars to show themselves. Under this Arctic sky we joined Anun at the simple camper's table and quietly partook of the mysterious though splendid stew. When he had finished, he rose, and with curt " 'nite" disappeared into one of the two yurts reserved for quarters. Young Culverson and I would share the third.

CHAPTER 12

Young Culverson awakened first, and hastened my awakening by saying: "Looks like Anun's up and gone already. Wonder what he's up to?"

The query focused my rising consciousness, so I ventured a rather groggy: "Maybe he's gone back over to the rig to check things out?"

"Don't think so. His hoverod's still here. Where ever he is, he's gone on foot."

The unexpected revelation finalized my waking, and sitting up on the air bed, I saw young Culverson's backside as he exited the yurt through the door flap. I stretched a little, to get some circulation in my nocturnally static lymph system and some fresh blood to my muscles and organs. Dressing quickly, I exited the yurt in search of young Culverson. I found him sitting at the camp table, an abundant portion of the ubiquitous morning scramble on his plate, and a hot tin cup of coffee in hand. He looked up at me and smiled a contrived pleasure in his meal. He said:

"Well, at the least he thought of us before he left. Scrambled eggs and coffee on the stove." He jutted his chin in the direction of the camp stove, and added: "Of course, leaving us something like *this*, it's hard to know what he was really thinking!" Young Culverson chuckled at his own wit.

"I'm ready to get to work," I said, while plopping a hearty portion of the scramble onto a tin camp plate, and pouring myself of cup of the black, morning liquor. "We've got to see if any of this tissue matches what we found at the pit."

Young Culverson nodded his agreement while shoveling another mass of the scramble in his mouth.

"Why don't you take a look under the microscope while I start extracting genetic material?"

Again young Culverson nodded his agreement, this time as he gulped at the dark and stimulating brew.

We finished our breakfast in silence, save for those unavoidable biologically sonances that naturally accompany deglutition and ingurgitation, both of our minds intent upon the immediate course of our research.

Once in the lab, I immediately apportioned the samples from the core rig. I would subject my portions to biochemical analyses, while young Culverson took the mechanical route, and would determine the structure of the tissues.

We had scarcely begun our respective inquiries when in a rather excited voice young Culverson began a soliloquy so laced with exclamations that I was at once distracted and attracted. I held my ground momentarily, and listened.

"This is incredible!.... Oh, I can't believe this!.... I've never seen anything like this…. "

He was so immersed in his continuing revelations that he seemed to have forgotten I was in the same room with him, or even the same universe, for that matter. I had no choice but to invite myself to intrude! I tried to be as exclamatory as he:

"My God, man! What are you looking at! Some sort of alien life form?!" I would later discover just how close to the truth that query was.

"Oh….oh! I'm sorry! I…well, I just can't quite figure what I'm looking at…I mean, it's not like anything I've seen before!"

His excitement was barely contained has he lunged into an explanation.

"Some of it's just like the tissue we found at the pit… on the outside. Like skin, maybe. But once you get to the deeper layers, well, the complexity increases exponentially!" He stopped to take a breath. "I mean, I've got cells here that have multiple nuclei; I've got what looks to be cells inside of cells; I've got structures like I never saw in any biology class!" He turned to me with a quite quizzical expression on his face. "This is going to take some sorting out. I mean, some *real* sorting out!"

I could contain my curiosity no longer: "Are you saying that maybe we're looking at some kind of absolutely new species?"

"Absolutely new!?? Absolutely incredible!!!"

"Okay…So, give me a layer by layer account." I wanted to calm him enough to get a good idea of the structures he was looking at so that I could better anticipate what I would find once I got back to my own investigation.

"Well, like I said, the outermost layer of cells are identical to the tissue making up the tubes we found at the pit. Right below them there seem to be layers of electrocytes…you know, like in the electric organs of eels. Between these layers are long thin cells containing what look like giant cellular tubules, with like swarms of mitochondria attached at their ends. On the deepest layer in the sample, there are some cells with multiple nuclei that contain cells with multiple nuclei…I mean, not like *anything* I've ever heard about or seen."

"Electrocytes, you say?" I waited to ask my question until he had finished his little dissertation, not wanting to disturb his train of thought. "An electric organ? That could explain the discharge… But how big would the organ have to be to produce a discharge as powerful as the one that apparently happened here?" I saw by the intensely cogitative knit on young Culverson's brow that he was not yet prepared to make this speculation. I let him off the hook.

"Okay. You work on that for bit. I'm more anxious than ever to see what my analysis turns up." I was soon as astounded as my young cohort.

I first went for the RNA, as that had been the most puzzling aspect in my analysis of the tissue from the pit. In order to extract RNA from most organisms one must first decompose the extant DNA. That had not been a problem at the pit because there was no DNA in the sample. In preparing for this extraction, however, I encountered DNA in such prodigious quantities that I found myself mentally reeling in trying for an explanation. I had taken a vertical sample of the tissue from the cutting teeth of the bit, and now realized this must represent the cells young Culverson found to have cells within cells with multiple nuclei. A further investigation determined a prodigious amount of ATP. I decided to do a simple spectrum analysis of the cell fluids. After centrifuging and removing the solids, a simple spectrum analysis showed an incredibly high percentage of heavy water. Usually high concentrations of heavy water are toxic to eukaryotic cells, but these cells seemed to have suffered no ill effects.

The day progressed rapidly, with one profound discovery after another. It was only the sudden onset of hunger pangs that brought me out of my disquisitive reverie. Looking toward young Culverson, I saw him slumped on a stool in front of the portable electron microscope, hands on his knees, head bowed either in fatigue or defeat. I hailed him.

"It's getting late. Let's get something to eat."

He rotated his head without lifting it so that the countenance he presented was horizontal, as if laying on a pillow. He shook his head slightly, and then righting himself, responded in a voice echoing something between awe and defeat: "I don't know what I'm looking at here." The plaintiff look in his eyes begged me to relieve him from his confusion. I could not; I could only distract.

"I'm going for food! That's one problem I can solve!.....I wonder if Anun's back from his wanderings?"

This new question seemed to emancipate young Culverson from his cryptic demons. "Yeah, I wonder where he got off to? And yes, I am famished. I've fired so many neurons today that I've lost weight – literally!"

Without further exchange, we quickly secured our devices and samples, exited the laboratory yurt, and headed for the camp mess.

The camp mess was quite an ingenious affair – an aluminum foldout that contained cooking, refrigeration, dry storage and seating, with lighting. Everything was gas/electric, supplied from replaceable canisters or solar panels that also served as a weather canopy. I went right to work, grabbing a couple of pouches of dehydrated stock, and putting them into water to boil. I didn't ask young Culverson if he had preferences, as I didn't believe it would matter given past experience with the menu.   Young Culverson went to work preparing some tea, nonchalantly combining the contents of several different colored packets. It was to be a custom brew. He looked at me and smiled, not for my approval, but rather at his creativity.

"The sun is getting low. Doesn't look like our headman is coming back this evening." My remark was as much query as statement.

"He's Inuit. This is his country. I don't think we have anything to worry about." Young Culverson was not attempting to alleviate any concerns I might have, just stating facts as he saw them.

"Yes. You're right. He's probably more at home out there than he would be here." I emphasized my point by jutting my chin in the direction of his supposed travel.

We conversed little during our meal, and after finishing, cleaning-up, and securing the mess against ursine marauders, retired to our yurt, to pass the short Arctic summer's night bathed in the somnolent undulations of the borealis, and immersed in what promised to be fantastic dreams.

CHAPTER 13

Morning intruded through the translucent skin of the inflated yurt, bringing me up from dreams that had been as fantastical as I had hoped, or feared. I awoke with an otherworldly sensation I had not known before. While contemplating its nature, I was suddenly greeted by the clanking of metal utensils. I looked quickly in the direction of young Culverson's sleeping sack and saw that it was still occupied. My first thought was *bears*! I grabbed a flare gun from the survival kit attached just inside the yurt's door flap, thinking to startle the intruders into submission and retreat if need be. It was not a plan I had ever practiced, but the exigencies of the moment offered no superior solution.

Armed with the now loaded gun, I slowly pulled back the yurt's door flap and peered out. There, at the camp mess, was our headman Anun, busily preparing the unescapable morning scramble and the attendant inky concoction that passed for coffee. He must have sensed my presence, for he turned immediately.

"Best give young Culverson a poke! Breakfast's 'bout done." He turned back to his work.

I did as instructed, and gently nudging young Culverson with a toe, brought him strugglingly up from his own carnival of nocturnal imagery.

"Anun's back. He's got breakfast." I turned and exited the yurt, leaving young Culverson blinking and shaking away the night's apparitions.

I took a seat at the mess's table, just as Anun slid a plate full of the scramble and a steaming cup of the morning's brew. He said nothing, put eyed the door flap of our yurt just as young Culverson emerged. He immediately began to prepare a portion of the breakfast menu for the now arriving lad. Then, fixing a portion for himself, he took a seat directly opposite me and began to consume his food voraciously. We three ate in silence, every nonverbal hint from the headman demanding it. When he had finished, he raised his head and looked directly into my eyes.

"Nanuq has come to me." He did not blink; he did not waver in his stare.

My mind raced to find an appropriate reply. I knew of his shamanism. I knew that Nanuq was the name the Inuit gave to the *Master of the Polar Bears*. I knew that it was part god to them; part guiding spirit. It emphasized the importance of the great white bears to their existence and culture. I could not answer lightly – flippantly. Fortunately, I could see the patience in the headman's eyes as I searched for an answer. Young Culverson, sensing the suspense, stopped with fork halfway to mouth, and also awaited my response. It was a long time coming.

How was I to take Anun's statement. He was a man scientifically trained – a superb engineer! And yet, he was Inuit, and a shaman to his people. I relied on scientific method to frame my response.

"You have seen Nanuq? A great white bear?"

"Yes. He came to me as I sat next to my fire. He walked upright, like a man, and like a man sat upon his haunches, his great forepaws held wide against the background of stars and *aksarnerk*, the great lights of the northern sky."

He spoke so earnestly and matter-of-factly that my scientific perspective felt challenged. I continued cautiously.

"Nanuq – he was an apparition, or a real bear?"

The headman showed no offense at the implications of my question.

"He was Nanuq! He is the great white bear that roams the vastness of our land, Nunavut; he is the great white bear that speaks to our minds, and lives in our hearts. Was he *real*, you are asking me? I tell you *yes*. As real as the sounds and images that now transmit from *your* senses to *your* mind telling you *I* am real."

Anun's scientific mind had analyzed the encounter, and found no better explanation. His Inuit heart had given him truth. I could not want for a better witness to such an event, save I should see it for myself. As if reading my mind, Anun, pronounced my thoughts.

"You, of course, wish to see Nanuq, as well."

There was not a hint of question in Anun's statement. It was as flat and formulaic as stating the chemical make-up of water.

"Yes! Of course! Is that possible?!" My excitement bounced off the headman's stoic countenance like a rubber ball off of a brick wall.

"First, you must prepare. Nanuq spoke to my mind, and told me these things: That there was another who should come, but that this other must prepare himself, for few men understand the true nature of things. The truth can blind the man that is not prepared to see." Anun looked at me with shaman eyes, and continued. "If you will avoid the madness that descended upon the others, you must first know many things…" The headman let his voice trail off. His averted eyes and fixed stare told me he was considering what must come next. "You understand what you have found?" he ask gravely, knowing full well that I, or rather young Culverson and I, were still grappling with that reality.

"No…No, not at all. We've just scratched the surface. We hardly have the equipment here to be definitive." My confession made not the slightest change in the headman's composure or delivery.

"Then we must return to Garry Lake, and perhaps to Bakers Lake. You must not pursue what comes next until you understand what already lays in your hands." With that the headman turned away, and immediately began to clear and clean our breakfast remains in preparation for collapsing the camp mess. I turned to young Culverson.

"Well, he's right. There's really not much more we can do here. Best secure the lab equipment and samples, and get ready to break camp. We should be able to make Bromley Lake today, and Garry Lake by tomorrow evening. I'll radio ahead to the pit and tell them to pack up and be ready to leave."

Young Culverson nodded an agreement. Without further conversation, and only the minimum necessary communication, we packed the equipment, deflated the yurts, and loaded everything onto the hoverods.

CHAPTER 14

The trip back to the pit, and thence to Garry Lake proved uneventful. Though the lab modules at Garry Lake were well equipped, they were insufficient to the task at hand. We opted to remain, but had to send samples back to Bakers Lake, some of which we knew would have to be forwarded to advanced research facilities at the lower latitudes. As the delay ran into several weeks, I spent considerable time with the headman, seeking his wisdom and understanding, as both an engineer and a shaman.

During this interlude I had the opportunity to go over transcripts of conversations between rescuers and authorities who had first contact with the drill team that had been found wandering and dazed far from their drill rig. Initial reports indicated that the individuals were amnesiac, not remembering anything that had transpired over the several preceding days. What was most interesting, however, was their common sense of having been dreaming, just unable to remember what they had been dreaming about. Subsequent examinations and interviews by psychiatrists and psychologists revealed that the effects of their experience had long term implications. The subjects seemed detached, even uncertain in their relationships with their closest family and friends. They continually requested to be together, and when they were, their conversations were about recurring thoughts and dreams. Not surprisingly, a polar bear was one of the frequent apparitions in their dreams. What was surprising was that they also described what were obviously sabre toothed tigers, wooly mammoths, mastodons, and giant sloths. As time passed their dreams seemed to take a devolutionary turn – one subject describing what were obviously dinosaurs; another describing an underwater world full of leviathans. All of the men experienced increasing anxiety and paranoia; increasing reclusiveness. Eventually all had to be institutionalized. The last recorded exchange had one of the subjects describing a steaming, sulfurous, caustic world devoid of life, in which he kept slipping into deep cracks in the earth.

Armed with the information in the reports, I wanted to compare the experiences they detailed with the headman's experience during his solo expedition beyond the rig site. We spoke regularly on a first name basis now, so I didn't hesitate to approach him with my query.

"Anun, you've read the reports?"

He smiled a small, rather devilish smile, and almost jocularly responded: "It's time we talk – yes? I've read the reports." He looked at me with squinted, teasing eyes, and continued: "You're gonna' find this hard to believe….but I'll give it to you straight. Let's take a walk over by the lake.

Someone overhears us here, and they're gonna' be spooked." Again the devilish grin.

I followed the headman across a small, open patch of tundra that lay between the camp modules and a small inlet from the lake. Someone had at some time past requisitioned old packing crates made of a rather tenacious composite material and constructed a long-backed bench within a meter of the shore. Most often the place was used for fishing; we would be trawling for much more than Arctic char.

The headman took a seat upon the bench, and immediately began plucking at the low tundral vegetation. He tossed choice bits onto the water's surface, which quickly attracted the attention of small fish, and created a small feeding frenzy. I took a seat next to him and quietly waited for him to begin the discourse.

"Ya' know, I got a degree in engineering 'cause from the time I was a boy I was fascinated by the white man's machines. I saw that science was a way to understand the world in a different way than my people. So I learned the white man's science well, and with it learned to do marvelous things. But in the end it does not give me a better truth than the customs of my people. Ya' see, the Inuit know that this world is to live in and to marvel at, but can't ever be completely known." The headman finished his soliloquy and went back to tossing bits of vegetation, or perhaps bugs, onto the water's surface. It was my turn.

"So, what do you think?....Tell me about your encounter with Nanuq." No use beating around the bush. He and I both new it was the purpose of our conversation.

"I walked nearly a day to the northeast, in the direction where the lost men were found. The farther I went, the more peculiar I felt. I kept tellin' myself it was just the old Inuit superstitions creepin' in. Had that feelin' like I was bein' watched, ya' know." He looked at me with squinted eyes again, but this time to measure the credibility I was giving to his story. Satisfied that I was listening objectively and honestly, he continued.

"I kept tellin' myself ain't nothin' here but me and the tundra and the bugs. But the feelin' kept growin'. Keep growin', like a buzz in my head. It got hard for me to concentrate. My mind kept driftin' off onto strange things. I was sure I was beginnin' to hallucinate, but I couldn't figure the cause. I had brought one of the gas and vapor samplers with me, but it didn't show any monoxides or nitrous compounds or anything common that might cause hypoxia or neurotoxicity. Air seemed completely clean. I couldn't see nothing'; couldn't smell nothin'. I began to panic a little. And I wanted to sleep. So I pitched a small camp and lit a fire cannister and crawled into my bag, not knowin' if I'd wake up or not, but not carin' by this point. I went out so fast, I don't remember layin' my head down."

Anun's account held to the scientific, which I appreciated. Even so, his story became harder and harder to explain by scientific principles – at least the ones with which I was familiar.

"I don't know how long I slept, or if in fact I did. But suddenly I had the sense someone had called my name, and I sat up, not groggy or anythin' from sleep, but acutely aware. The fire from the canister was still burnin' so I knew I hadn't slept more 'n four hours, or it would've extinguished. The Borealis was brilliant, so I had a good view of the horizon, and I could immediately make out a figure comin' my way. It was upright, but its lumberin', swayin' movement made it immediately evident it was not a man – at least not like us. For a moment I thought: *"My God! It's Tornit! The Bigfoot!"* My heart started to pound and I tried to focus on it. Then it entered the circle of yellow light cast by the canister fire, and I saw immediately that it was a great white bear! My emotions went from somethin' near panic to absolute fear! I tried to rip myself out of the sleeping bag, but my hurried efforts only snaggled the zipper. As I struggled with it, a terrible sense of resignation came over me. I could not look at the bear. I knew that momentarily its massive claws and teeth would reach my flesh. I closed my eyes, acceptin' my fate, hopin' that bein' eaten by a bear would not be as horrible as I imagined; hopin' the bear would dispatch me with one great strike of its paw, or a single vicious bite to my neck. I stopped breathin', trying to make myself go unconscious before the encounter."

The headman halted his narrative and once again turned to me, searching my countenance for indications that I understood the full terror of his experience. Obviously satisfied, he bent down and snatched another piece of foliage and tossed it onto the water. He began again.

"I had begun my death chant. My Inuit heart now found comfort only in the traditions of my people. I abandoned the white man's science for the solace of my Inuit spirit." He paused briefly, keeping his head down. Then, suddenly lifting his head and looking out across the lake, he resumed his story.

"The bear did not come. I waited for the strike, tryin' to relax in my faith, but every muscle tense, every nerve alert, every sense acute. But nothin'! And then suddenly the sound of somethin' heavy droppin' to the ground. Half in terror, half in hope, I turned toward the bear." Here again he paused, evidently wanting to make sure I had time to digest all the information he had recounted.

"The great bear sat on its haunches across the fire from me. So much adrenaline flowed in my veins, so many emotions struggled for precedence, and yet my rationale mind also fought for its place. I couldn't tell for sure if the bear was real, or hallucination. The same buzzin' sensation in my head that had compelled me to camp, now reverberated to a roar. The bear was lookin' me square in the eyes, it's paws outstretched. But the eyes lookin' at me were more than a bear's eyes – they had questions in them. I don't know how to explain it any better – they had *questions*!"

Anun stopped again, this time obviously to reassess his words; to make sure they were carrying the right message, the right emphasis. I took this opportunity to question him.

"So you say you think the bear might have been a hallucination? Did you have any physical sensations that might indicate it was real?"

The headman responded quite scientifically. "You and I both know hallucinations can involve all the senses. The addict who thinks he's bein' eaten by spiders is in as much pain as you or I would be in a pit of tarantulas." He paused, and then: "But there was the smell…..like the smell of the sea and ice….No, I don't think it was an hallucination…..I believe it was a real bear. I could hear it breathing…"

We both sat quietly for moment, each giving the other time to contemplate the implications that a real bear presented. The suddenly Anun began again.

"But I can't be certain, because other strange things began to happen. Memories started floodin' into my consciousness – I remembered huntin' great white bears with my father; I remembered the fear and the excitement; I remembered my father saying a prayer for the bears' spirits after he shot them. And all the while the bear was there lookin' at me, and I felt like he was seein' the memories too!"

A moment of silenced ensued, but then I had to ask: "Do you think the bear was having a telepathic communication with you?" It was a far-fetched question, I knew, but one that an honest scientific investigation had to ask. The headman's answer was more surprising than my question.

"No, I don't think it was the bear I was communicatin' with. I think somethin' was usin' the bear to communicate with me!"

With this remark, Anun turned to me with an absolutely open expression on his face. He was obviously hoping I might offer some reasonable explanation for his experience – or at least a reasonable speculation. I had none. He nodded slightly in acceptance of my silence, and raised his eyebrows as he resumed his tale.

"Somethin' had got inside my head. I don't know how. Telepathy? Well, there ain't no science to support it. Spirits? I'm Inuit, but not ignorant. To me, spirits live in the mind, yes, but they don't control worldly things – but just the hearts and minds of men from within. I got to tell ya' – it was frightenin', not havin' control over my own thoughts. I tried talkin' to myself but images in my head just kept comin' and comin'! Everything – memories from every part of my life. Memories I didn't even know I had, but which I knew were absolutely true once I remembered them – or IT remembered them for me! I can understand how them riggers got so messed up. They were caught out there for days! After a few minutes, I was nearly crazy!" The headman paused for a moment, then continued: "Then suddenly my mind cleared. I was lookin' straight at the bear, and I could see the change in his eyes too! It fell over backwards in a start, as if it was just seein' the fire, and once it got to its feet, took off on all fours like it was terrified, lookin' back several times to make sure I – or something – wasn't chasin' it."

The headman fell silent again. I wasn't prepared to ask any further questions yet – the information I was trying to analyze had my mind whirling. He began again, and I could tell by his demeanor, and the resignation in his voice that these would be his final words on the matter.

"I've got enough education to know how the world's supposed to work. This don't fit that picture at all. I don't know what happened out there, but I know that I don't want no more of it!"

He turned to me again, this time with all the wisdom and warning of a shaman burning in his eyes.

"I don't know what you're plannin' – but I can tell you this: Don't send no one else out there till you know for certain what you're dealin' with. I'm not gonna' be over this for a while; don't suspect those riggers will ever be over it. Maybe it's somethin' we're not supposed to know. Doesn't sound so scientific, I know."

With that Anun slapped the open palms of his hands on the tops of his legs, stood up and began to walk back in the direction of the labs. After a few paces, he stopped and turned, and offered this last statement: "Don't expect no help from the Inuit." And then turned and continued on his way.

I sat for nearly an hour contemplating the headman's story, occasionally escaping to enjoy the ever brightening Borealis in the darkening sky. By the time I got back to the labs, only young Culverson could be found, sitting alone in the mess.

CHAPTER 15

The sudden departure of the Inuit headman was a complication that neither I nor young Culverson had anticipated. At breakfast the next morning, sitting at our usual table away from the rest, it became evident from the persistent and agitated conversations of the remaining Inuit workers that we would soon be facing a mass exodus. The stories about the core rig workers, all who had been Inuit but the one survivor, and he being a "white man", sparked fears among the indigenous folks that they had somehow trespassed against the native spirits and were being singled out for retribution. The obvious unsettling of their headman and his immediate departure without explanation had them all ready to bolt. Young Culverson spoke first.

"I've communicated with my uncle. He's going to try to round up some help for us, but with so much activity going on south of here, it may prove difficult. The actions moving north, but we're still at the leading edge of it."

I nodded in reply as I took up another spoonful of the morning fare. The usual scramble had been replaced by a type of hash that was probably better suited to the canine diet. But with a little hot coffee it was sufferable. I could see the

Inuit were still feasting on the scramble, and so I imagined they had requisitioned the remaining stock as part of their severance pay.

Young Culverson and I were correct in our supposition. After finishing breakfast, we had gone straight to the labs to continue our analysis, and to see if any reports had arrived from the lower latitudes. Just as we were settling into work, one of the Inuit workers entered, and without hesitation or apology, informed of his and his fellows' intent.

"We're leavin' now. We won't take no hovercraft, just some supplies. Hope you fella's know what you're doin'." Then with only the slightest nod, he turned and exited. I followed, and caught the door before it closed.

The Inuit had constructed travois out of metal tubing and nylon strapping, and had loaded them with necessary supplies – foodstuffs, fire canisters, and an inflatable yurt. With additional nylon strapping they harnessed themselves in like sled dogs, and leaning slightly into their loads made off in a southerly direction, never once looking back. Though nothing could be seen in that direction except the gentle undulations of tundra spotted with myriad reflections of sky from the multitude of small lakes and ponds, I was certain they knew exactly where they were going.

I had just returned to my work when young Culverson approached. He was obviously carrying on some intense interior dialogue, as he nearly collided with me before realizing he had reached his destination.

"I've been looking hard at this cell within cell structure," he began, seeming oblivious to our near collision. "And it's starting to look like the interior cells are some kind neurocyte, and the majority of the cells surrounding them some kind of astrocyte, like the whole inside of the thing is just a big nervous system. Just like the cells from the surface tissue, they all seem to be interconnected, though. Just under the surface cells are a layer of cells that look to be the origin of the bioelectricity, and then a layer of the cells containing the tubules and what appear to be mitochondria. I've managed to separate enough of each layer to give you a good sample for analysis." He handed me four labeled sample vials. "I'm gonna' try to separate a sample of the spindle structures to see if I can figure out what's going on there." Then, as absentmindedly as he has approached, he turned and headed back to his work area.

I took the samples young Culverson had given me and immediately set out to extract DNA from each tissue level, to determine why so much of it seemed present. Again I was surprised at the mass of nucleic acid harvested, particularly from the glial like astrocytes. I took that sample to the electron microscope, and was astounded by what I saw! The mass of the DNA was not the result of longer strands, or even more strands than might be anticipate, but by the fact that all but a small of amount of the DNA was not the double-helix found in most modern life forms on Earth, but rather consisted of strands that were multiplex, and by that I mean triplex and quadraplex and octaplex - it appeared to go up to at least dodecahex – twelve spirals of nucleic polymer! Beyond that the material became so entangled it was not possible to tell if higher orders of complexity existed, or merely combinations of the identifiable multiplexes. I was just beginning to put some order to my speculations when young Culverson made another appearance. He began talking several paces before reaching me, but in a voice loud enough to catch my attention.

"Okay, the ATP is coming from the cells with tubules. It's moving between cells via the plasmodesmata, I guess, because there's no circulatory system, and the other cells don't seem to have any mechanism for producing it – just moving across a concentration gradient. I've isolated some of the tubules. They're made of protein, but seem to be filled with heavy water and palladium, of all things! So I don't know where the energy is coming from for ATP synthesis. I mean, plants use sunlight to knock electrons loose, and that energy is used to synthesize ATP which in turn provides the energy to produce sugar. And we breakdown sugar to harvest energy to produce the ATP that runs all the process in our bodies. But I don't see what's going on here. I've already sent my results down to my uncle at Bakers Lake.

Maybe he can figure it out, or find someone that can. Maybe results will come in soon from the samples we sent down. Till then, I don't know what to do next." Young Culverson had executed his complete narration so rapidly, and with so few breathes he was left panting. I had nothing more than additional quandaries to offer as he caught his breath.

"I'm sort of at a dead end too. Most of the DNA I'm finding is extremely multiplexed, which doesn't make any sense when we're looking at something with so little structure. I mean, what could all that coding be for? So far we've got something not much more biologically complex than a jellyfish, or perhaps a fungus. How many genes does it take to code for that?"

The rather blank look on young Culverson's face informed me that not only had I not succeeded in easing his consternation, but that I had merely added mine to it. His next suggestion was really the only reasonable solution.

"Why don't we give it up for today? Right now some of that hash and hot cup of coffee seems a reasonable thing to do. And there's a jug of ethanol in the chemical locker that two chemically adept fellows like ourselves could surely put to a more creative and congenial use." Young Culverson ended his proposition with a Shakespearian flourish.

CHAPTER 16

I suppose it was the allusion to the Avonian Bard mixed with the alcohol and the quandaries inherent in the day's discoveries that resulted in a midsummer's Arctic night filled with the strangest of dreams. If dreams truly reflect insight, then I was on a collision course with astral octopi, undulating, boreal jellyfish, and talking mushrooms as clever and evanescent as the Cheshire cat. Even my scientific perspective and lyrical proclivity seemed to have melded into a single, formless whole - my adult self and my grammar school avatar made one. I awoke certain that I knew something, and was ready to immortalize it in poetic phrase. Yet, as the interior of my quarters came into focus, the insight, the understanding, the inspiration vanished, replaced by the bitter cotton left in my mouth by excess ethanol and excessive dehydration. It took a bit to establish a good sense of my location and purpose, but directly a snorting and gulping from the yet supine form of young Culverson brought back certain visages of the previous night's alcoholic debauchery.

Stress often finds relief in the form of a disproportionate indulgence, in this case the ethanol, the jug of which I believed we had nearly managed to consume. It was an attempt to silence an inner scientific argument that had become so intense and yet so seemingly inscrutable that young Culverson and I were forced into retreat, at least momentarily. Not disturbing my obviously still recovering partner in debauchery, I made my way to mess hall, looking for some water to ease the dehydration, and some of the black potion to counteract the post-inebrial lethargy.

Stepping into the daylight, I immediately noted the sun indicated very late morning. Scanning the area I also immediately noticed a new hovercraft sitting in the space in front of the mess hall. We had obviously had arrivals sometime between submitting to unconsciousness and my rather groggy resurrection. I quickened my pace to the mess hall.

Stepping from the daylight into the artificial light of the mess hall caused a momentary blindness as my retinae dilated to accommodate the lower level of light. As the interior came into view, I saw that Davison Culverson sat at one of the tables, studying the readouts on a compuscroll. Aware of my entrance, he held of a finger to keep me silent while he finished a passage. Then he turned to me, with a mischievous grin.

"I would have awakened you, but the place smelled and sounded like a Bakers Lake detox unit, so I thought it best to let you sleep." His pretense at an apologetic smile only deepened his sarcasm.

"Yes…well. We've had a tough few weeks up here. Needed to let of a little steam." I was not offended by his remarks; he nodded full agreement with mine. He looked back at the compuscroll and began to speak.

"I've got reports here on the samples you sent down....Some incredible stuff here!" He looked directly at me to emphasize his emphasis. "I mean, not like anything anyone has ever seen...Oh, by the way, got some coffee brewed over there. I brought some fresh provisions with me, so there eggs – *real* eggs – and toast if you want it.

Though my stomach objected, the thought of eating a real egg was just too inviting, so I headed to the food line to check out the offering. I returned with a great mound of fluffy fresh scrambled eggs, several pieces of lavishly buttered toast, a handful of jam packets, and a steaming mug of what smelled to be genuine coffee.

"Fresh coffee too?!" I queried mockingly.

"Yeah, brought some of my private stash of beans. Got to take good care of the help!" He smiled, then continued. "Speaking of help....looks like I'm it. The rumors about what's going on up here are flying all over Nunavut. The Inuits absolutely refuse to consider returning. They've pretty well spooked everyone else as well."

I took a seat opposite Davison Culverson, and began to consume the fare cautiously, my enthusiasm for fresh food well-tempered by the lingering effects of the alcohol. Davison Culverson returned to scanning the compuscroll, giving me a rundown of the contents of the reports.

"You're right about the absence of DNA in the samples from the pit. Also about the presence of ATP with no associated synthases or structures. The general consensus from the experts is that it is some sort of extremely primitive organism that's getting its ATP from some external source. They agree that it could very well represent something close to LUCA, the last universal common ancestor." He looked up to see that I had digested the information successfully, and even though he caught me stuffing another spoonful of eggs in my mouth, was satisfied that I understood the implications.

"Now here comes the interesting part: The tissue was obviously secreting solvating substances, most probably hydrochloric acid and hydrogen cyanide, again from sources unknown, and absorbing salt solutions, primarily chlorides and cyanides of palladium. No mechanisms for transport could be detected in the tissue, though the presence of plasmodesmata suggest transport is gradient driven."

I had finished the eggs, and was delighting in toast and jam with a second cup of real java, so I was not inclined to proffer questions as of yet. Davison Culverson continued.

"So, at the pit we've got what appears to be evidence for a very primitive, prokaryotic, multicellular organism utilizing RNA, operating on ATP, and capable of transporting various solutions – but to what purpose? Well, the second report gets even *curiouser!*" Obviously Davison Culverson had had a Carrollian grammar school experience similar to mine.

Just as he was about to address the second report, a sudden flash of light at the mess hall door indicated the arrival of young Culverson. His backlit figure hesitated at the entrance as he also waited for his vision to acclimate. Once he spotted us, and recognized his uncle, his face broke into a wide, delighted smile.

"Uncle Davison! When did you get here? What a surprise! I thought you'd send help. Didn't realize you'd be coming yourself!" Young Culverson's rapid fire greeting belied the bloodshot, alcoholic lethargy that swam over his eyes and slightly slurred his speech.

Davison Culverson rose to greet his nephew, giving him a robust embrace. "Kid, you look like hell! No wonder everyone's afraid to come up here!" Young Culverson took the jab at his hungover appearance with a shrug and a sheepish smile. "Better get something inside of you before your insides come out!" his uncle continued with another good natured barb. He steered young Culverson in the direction of the food line. "Don't worry, you won't miss out on anything. I'll wait till you get back to start on the second report."

"The *second* report!" Young Culverson feigned injury in having obviously missed the first report.

"The world doesn't wait for a man to sleep it off." With this final barb, Davison Culverson gave his nephew a push in the direction of his breakfast. When he was out of ear shot, Davison confided to me: "I took the boy under my wing when my brother died. But he's never quite got over it. Just buries himself in his work...well, most of the time, when he's in *good* company!" This barb was directed at me. I pretended an arrow to the back which amused the older Culverson. We sat and sipped at coffee until young Culverson returned with his plate and cup.

"So, did I miss much in the first report?"

I spoke up: "No, the experts came to pretty much the same conclusions we did."

Young Culverson was satisfied with my response, and taking his seat, encouraged his uncle. "Well, let's get on with the second report. I hope it deals with the findings at the drilling site. The things we found there have got my brain as scrambled as these eggs!"

"Well, if you think your stomach is settled enough, I'll gladly begin." I'm sure that comment was directed to me as much as to young Culverson. Davison Culverson swept his fingers across the compuscroll, and began to divulge its contents.

"First things first – the tissue found at the pit is the same as some of the tissue found at the drill site. But the other tissues found – well...where to begin!" Davison Culverson threw up a hand at this exclamation. I supposed he was trying to prepare us for what came next. "You were spot on about the bioelectric nature of some of the tissue. You were also correct in your analysis of the nested cells as appearing to be neurocytes. They have dendrites connecting them via the plasmodesmata to surrounding cells. They also seem to be the source of the bioelectric effect. As to why their nuclei contain such an abundance of multiplexed DNA can't be determined. It certainly isn't necessary for the replication of the cells themselves. But here's the one that's really gonna' get'cha..." Davison Culverson paused and took a long, slow draught of his coffee. Glancing at both his nephew and me to see that he had effectively tantalized us, he continued.

"You were also right about the abnormal concentration of heavy water. Seems it's not so unusual to encounter a slightly greater concentration of heavy water in the thaw layers of the permafrost, as it freezes before regular water does, so gets trapped in the layer while the water continues to migrate...But the concentrations in the tissue were incredible! So, obviously the organism, if we want to call it that, has a way of collecting the heavy water from the layer. But why?" Again Davison Culverson paused, this time searching through the documents on the compuscroll, obviously looking for something in particular. Young Culverson and I took the opportunity to exchange glances, and compare our relative astonishment. Directly, Davison Culverson began again.

"They had to call in a biophysicist on this one. I expect you're gonna' find this as difficult to accept as I did – as the biophysicist still does!" Not wanting to outrun our understanding of what was being suggested, Davison Culverson asked his nephew to get us all another cup of coffee. While the younger Culverson was so engaged, he shared this little aside with me: "This is either gonna' get us written up as the greatest scientists of the twenty-second century, or as charlatans." His expression indicated he truly was not certain which the case would be.

Once refueled with hot java, Davison Culverson again began to divulge the contents of the second report. "They were able to successfully isolate the tubules in the cells surrounding the neurocytes. What they found is absolutely incredible! The fluid inside the tubules is somewhere around 90% pure heavy water. And floating around in this water are these very delicate matrices of palladium atoms. Now, as a geneticist and biologist, I can't make any sense of this. How about you two?" Both young Culverson and I shook our heads in the negative, not wanting to break Davison Culverson's revelations. "Well, bring in the physicist then! Seems that when you pair the contents of the tubules with rhythmic electrical pulses – like ones that can be provided by the bioelectric tissues – you get fusion!"

I knew all about fusion. I knew that after nearly two centuries men had only just begun to develop economically viable fusion reactors. And now we were being told that an organism perhaps as ancient as any life on Earth was using fusion! Fusion for what?! As if reading my mind, Davison Culverson continued.

"Yes, fusion! The release of energy – of quanta – by electrolyzing molecules of heavy water trapped in the palladium matrix under an induced current, and then forcing the free deuterium close enough for it to fuse into helium!"

I dared not look at young Culverson as the realization of what his uncle was saying swept over me. Being his elder, I was loathe to have him see the absolute state of incredulity I was sure that now beamed from my eyes. Davison Culverson took this opportunity to lean back in his seat and observe the effect of his pronouncements on his gallery. No doubt he enjoyed lavishing upon us the same revelations that had certainly robbed his innocence. Young Culverson put his head between his opened palms and pressed, either to prevent his head from exploding, or to assuage the pounding that surely the combination of alcoholic aftereffect and intellectual overload broadcast through his brain. Not done with us yet, Davison Culverson prepared the coup de grace.

"To what purpose? It seems the mitochondrial structures attached to the ends of the tubules contain molecules not unlike a chlorophyll, that when bombarded with low energy quanta, let loose electrons! Then there's the electron transport chain and synthase! It's photosynthesis! It's the source of the ATP!"

The dramatic gestures and the crescendo in Davison Culverson's voice as he delivered his pronouncements were worthy of any thespian. Yet the effect of his revelation on me is hard to put into words. It would be juvenile to admit that it was much like finding out that treasured childhood myths were suddenly discovered to be falsehoods. And yet it was. It would be disingenuous to say that I accepted the news with all the detachment and soberness of a scientific professional. And yet I tried. But the revelations so confounded me that I suddenly found myself falling down the rabbit hole!

On the face of it, what was so incredible? Life had found a way to obtain the essentials for its continuation and procreation in almost every niche of Earth's environment– on land and sea there was sunlight photosynthesis; in the rock and deep sea trenches there were chemo- and thermosynthesis. What would we call this? Fusiosynthesis? Nucleosynthesis? My speculations caused a small, nearly hysterical laugh to escape in response to my speculative nomenclature. I hoped no one noticed. Upon looking up, I saw that young Culverson was as flummoxed as I. Davison Culverson was sitting smugly, with arms crossed, obviously enjoying every moment of our discomfiture. He spoke.

"I know *exactly* how you feel!" His emphasis was his confession. "I still haven't been able to completely wrap my head around it! And, of course, some of the folks down south haven't and won't. They are certain that we are pranking them. If one of the tabloid apps gets ahold of it – well, I'm sure our professional careers will be over!"

This last precautionary musing brought a sudden soberness to my mental crapulence. Indeed, we were dealing with something here that represented such a paradigm shift, such an affront to the current dogma that we could certainly expect flak from the scientific community – and lots of it! But aside from that, what did it imply for this moment, in this place? What was the reasonable course of action? To doubt the findings, and spend time and energy re-examining the evidence? Or to proceed from this point by accepting the proposition, however farfetched it seemed, and move forward with the investigation? After all, there was still the phenomenon experienced by the rig workmen, and reinforced by the headman's experience. With all this whirling madly in my head, I cleared my throat and began to speak.

"I think we've got to take the next step. I mean, we've got two sites nearly thirty kilometers apart, and yet they're connected! And we've got another as yet unexplained phenomenon that may or may not be associated that's thirty kilometers farther on! Is this a whole population of organisms, or more incredibly, is this a single organism, like a fungal mycelium?"

"Or are WE being pranked?" I was sure Davison Culverson's dour interrogative was meant only to be precautionary. The look in his eyes projected the intense fire of the indefatigable adventurer. Neither young Culverson nor I gave the remark the smallest consideration.

"Okay then!" Davison Culverson slapped the table with his open hands, causing young Culverson to lose the final bite of breakfast that had for several moments now sat upon his hovering fork awaiting consumption. Instead of retrieving it, he tossed his fork on the plate, and spoke.

"Yes! We've got to get to the bottom of this! I say let's pack up and head on up to where the lost rig workers were found! We're not going to be able to put this puzzle together until we get all the pieces!"

In principle I agreed with young Culverson. Everything to this point indicated something so incredible, so beyond the bounds of current understanding that it did not seem unreasonable that the mental effects experienced by the rig workers, and then later by Anun, the headman, could be connected. But as I considered the prospects, the headman's warning came back to me: "Don't send no one else out there till you know for certain what you're dealin' with."

CHAPTER 17

We spent the next days reviewing the reports, and quizzing each other on the facts and implications. I expressed my concerns over the headman's warning. We made a list of the empirical data, and offered hypotheses. The sum of the matter still seemed something incredible: We agreed on designating the tissue as belonging to an organism. We agreed that the tissue from the pit and from the drill site were parts of similar organisms, or perhaps even the same organism. We agreed that the organism was an autotroph, and that as improbable as it seemed, a type of photosynthesis utilizing a fusion reaction was its mechanism. We did not agree on how related organisms, or a single organism could display primitive, LUCA like characteristics in one place, and multiplexed DNA in another. We did not agree on what purpose the multiplexed DNA served. We agreed on the organisms' or organism's bioelectric potential, and that it was the cause of the discharge at the drill site. We did not agree on whether the charge was accumulated from a collection of organisms, or was the product of a single organism. We agreed that the organisms or organism was widespread, perhaps like a colony of bacteria, or perhaps like the mycelium of a fungus.

We agreed that the cells containing cells most closely resembled the relationship between neurons and glial cells in known species. We did not agree whether such a collection or structure could be sentient. And it was here that argumentation ceased, and proposals for our next course of action began. Young Culverson offered the first suggestion.

"Why don't we just pack up and head in the direction Anun took, and see if we can duplicate his experience?"

A more cautious Davison Culverson made the next offering. "I met with some of the survivors from the exploratory crew that went missing. They have obviously suffered psychological damage, if not outright neurological damage. What happens if we go marching in there and get our brains scrambled?"

Remembering the headman's warning, I joined the conservative argument. "Your uncle is right. How much investigating are we going to get done if we end up comporting with polar bears? I think we have got to take a very measured approach here." Davison Culverson nodded his adamant support. Young Culverson responded with a query.

"So, how are we going to do this? Go in with aluminum foil wrapped around our heads?" His humor revealed his frustration, but planted a seed that quickly sprouted in my thoughts.

"That's it! According to Anun's readings there were no signs of biological or chemical hallucinogens present....That only leaves electromagnetic interference. Maybe it's something akin to what the government forces use for crowd control? You know...extremely low frequency EM waves that interrupt neuronal signals. I've seen videos of it being used! People stumbling around like zombies..."

"You mean we've got a creature here that can control our thoughts?!" Young Culverson's incredulity quickly faded to consternation as his brows knitted and his eyes narrowed as he considered the implications of what I had said.

Davison Culverson began a verbal analysis of those implications. "Well, we've certainly got what appears to be neuronal structure capable of generating charges. If these "neurons" are communicating across synapses, which they *could* be doing since they have dendrites extending through the plasmodesmata....This thing could be thinking! Maybe the electrical discharges and mental confusions are just defensive mechanism?" Davison Culverson's voice trailed off as he internalized his analysis. I picked up the argument and continued.

"Makes sense! So what we've got to do is get some equipment up here that can detect extremely low frequency EM waves!" I saw the light go on in the Culversons' eyes. We were agreed. Davison Culverson made the next offering.

"The only place close we might get that kind of equipment would be the RCMP post at

Bakers Lake. Their troopers wear sensing equipment so they can stay at a safe range during crowd control. Hate to say it, but they've already had to use it a few times to quell riots when the government office there issued homesteading and mineral rights. I know the Chief Superintendent. I'll send him a message."

Davison Culverson used his compuscroll to compose and transmit a message to the commandant. Then we continued discussing our next course of action. Young Culverson offered a very interesting point to consider.

"Supposing all of these parts *are* a single organism. It's got to be huge! Not only that, what form is it? Is it linear, like a snake, and we're moving from tail to head? Or could it be radial, like an octopus, and were moving from the tentacles to the head? Do you realize what that would mean?!" He began verbalizing some quick calculations. "From the pit to the place where the workers were lost is about sixty kilometers. Take that as the radius of a circle, and do a little πr^2…that's sixty squared is thirty six hundred times about three is…that's like over ten thousand square kilometers!!"

Young Culverson's calculations were good. If what we were encountering was in fact a single, radially splayed organism with hyphae like appendages gathering nutrients, or perhaps more correctly fusible elements, to an increasingly polykaryotic, encephalonic core, was it too incredible to imagine it might be sentient? That perhaps we could communicate with it? I kept these speculations to myself at the time, as they were scarcely believable to me, and I dared not injure my credibility with the Culversons.

As we sat contemplating our own versions of the circumstances, Davison Culverson's compuscroll chimed. He picked it up and read the message aloud:

> *From the office of the Chief Superintendent, RCMP-Nunavut: Due to the peculiar nature of your message it is requested that you make secure communications with this office ASAP.*

I wasn't sure what was meant by "secure communications", but it wasn't surprising that a man of Davison Culverson's importance should. Reaching into a black, ballistic bag under the table he retrieved a satellite communicator that was obviously of military origin. He touched its screen a few times which brought a quick, canned audio response.

"This is the Chief Superintendent's office. You are calling on a secure frequency. Please enter your clearance ID."

Davison Culverson tapped the screen a few times, and a boisterous but friendly voice came over the communicator.

"Davison, you old….Are we secure?"

"Chief Superintendent, I have the speaker on. My nephew and Dr. Bander are here with me. They have information important to my request." Davison Culverson kept everything formal, though it was evident they were personal friends. The Chief Superintendent responded in similar fashion.

"You've made a rather peculiar request. You care to explain a bit more than just '*checking out the source of possible induced hallucinations in your workers?*'

Young Culverson took the prompt, and without invitation, but an abundance of youthful enthusiasm not to be denied, began to recount the events leading up to the present circumstance.

"Chief Superintendent, I'm sure you know about the chemical burns, the electrocution accident and the lost workers…" He didn't wait for a reply. He knew, as well as I, that the reports we had read on these two events came from the RCMP. What he didn't know, nor did I, was that some of the reports Davison Culverson had shared with us from "experts" down south, were in fact reports from RCMP forensics labs. "Well, we think they're all related. We think we got some kind of giant organism up, like maybe ten thousand square kilometers…" The Chief Superintendent interrupted.

"Wait a minute. Wait a minute! Who's that talking? Davison, what's going on there! Are you all hallucinating!" The exasperation in the Chief Superintendent's voice, and the admonition written across Davison Culverson's face silenced his nephew.

"Sorry for that Chief Superintendent. My nephew is extremely excited about our find." The Chief Superintendent broke in again.

"About your *find*? I thought you were trying to trace down a possible source of EM induced hallucination. Now I'm hearing about some huge organism?!" There was both anxiety and agitation in the Chief Superintendent's voice. "Listen, whatever you've got going on up there – you keep it quiet! We've got people pouring into the territory by the thousands looking for whatever they can find. Many of them are coming because of the gold, but just as many are coming to take advantage of the miners. None of them come as prepared as they should for life this far north. They end up robbing and killing each other, or fighting over scraps. It's all we can do to keep the peace around here. Can you imagine what would happen if rumor got out about some giant creature living under the tundra?!" The Chief Superintendent's tone easily weighted his admonition. Davison Culverson responded in a conciliatory tone.

"If you don't mind, Chief Superintendent, I'm going to put Dr. Bander on. He's the best qualified of us. He can give you the best idea of what we think we are up against."

I was not particularly pleased with being put on the spot, but Culverson was correct is pointing out my expertise. As I gathered my thoughts, the Chief Superintendent spoke.

"Dr. Bander? You the one who wrote *Epidemiology and Climate Change*?" I was surprised – no, shocked that he would be familiar with my book. It was an extremely academic work that had only sold a few hundred copies as far as I knew (and as far as my royalties indicated), and then only to those colleagues I knew personally, and suspected had bought the book out of kindness.

"Yes, I am. I'm surprised you've heard of it. A rather dry, academic work, I'm afraid." I hoped I didn't come across as to self-deprecating. The Chief Superintendent's response was very matter of fact.

"Actually, we use excerpts in training our Emergency Medical Response Teams. Want them to take every precaution these days. Don't want any mutant bugs making rounds in Nunavut. Don't suppose this is some sort of mutant you've come up against, do you *doctor*?" His voice seemed joking until he pronounced my title, at which point it was quite obvious that he took the situation seriously.

"I don't think it's a mutant, though without the thaw we might never have encountered it. Actually, I'm beginning to think the thing is very ancient. I don't want to take off on a bunch of biology-speak, but from the samples we have we're seeing things that might be as ancient as the first life on Earth." The Chief Superintendent interjected with a question.

"If it's so damned ancient, what do you need ultra-low frequency detectors for? You telling me this thing's got a mind?!" Incredulity began to creep into the Chief Superintendents voice.

"Well, in a way, yes. Some of the tissue we found is definitely neurocytic – I mean, like nerves, like the cells our brains are made of. If its sentient, we might be able to pick up brain waves…" The Chief Superintendent's growing incredulity exploded in his next response.

"What are you saying? You saying you've got some kind of brain growing underground up there? Are you sure you aren't hallucinating *now*, doctor."

"I know how incredible this sounds. But that's only the beginning. The thing appears to be autotrophic – self-feeding –using a fusion reaction. And it's large." Somewhat submissively the Chief Superintendent posed his next question.

"Okay. How *large* is it"

Before I could answer young Culverson piped up. "Ten thousand square acres!" Young Culverson's response was met with silence. After an uncomfortable pause, I attempted an explanation.

"We think the organism has a network of hyphae like structures that it uses to gather nutrients, much like a fungal mycelium." The Chief Superintendent interrupted, the frustration evident in his voice.

"Fungus!? You mean like a mushroom? *You* think you've got a giant mushroom up there that *thinks*?!" His voice sounded confused, on the verge of anger. I continued.

"No! We don't think it's a mushroom. But we don't know *what* it is. I think we *have* to find out, though. If we could get one of your ultra-low frequency EM wave detectors – actually, if we could get a detector and one of your EM transmitters – I think we could go a long way towards understanding this thing."

The Chief Superintendent came back sarcastically. "What you going to do? Confuse it?!" Silence again. Then he started again, having obviously regained his composure. "You realize how incredible, how crazy this sounds?! He didn't wait for a response. "Okay, here's what I'll do. I'll send one of my techs, Constable Henry to you, with a transmitter and a detector. But you keep this under wraps. Culverson, you there?"

Davison Culverson sat up and acknowledged. "Yes, I'm here."

With all the authority of his office sounding in his voice, the Chief Superintendent pronounced his protocol. "I'm at this moment declaring this a classified matter! Any word of this gets out, and we get a rush a people up there, I'm going to hold you legally liable, understood?"

Responding as if a good soldier to his commanding officer, Davison Culverson offered crisply: "Yessir. Understood." The Chief Superintendent returned congeniality.

"All right, Davison. The Constable should be up there sometime tomorrow. Be careful. Maybe its alien, and looking for meal." The humor of this final remark did not bely the Chief Superintendent's care for our well-being. He broke off his end of the transmission.

The Culversons and I spent the rest of the afternoon provisioning the hovercraft for our trip back to the drill site and beyond. We agreed to each consider a plan of action while we worked, and to work out a plan over the evening meal.

CHAPTER 18

W e had decided on a preliminary plan over a dinner of broiled char caught out of Bromley Lake. We chased it with a little ethanol laced fruit juice, this time our consumption well-modulated. Over breakfast we fine-tuned our plan.

Not that I volunteered, but I did agree with the consensus that I was the best qualified to be point man as we continued. Constable Henry having not yet arrived, we volunteered him to be my wingman. We would advance to the northeast from the drill site until we detected, experienced, or suspected that we were within the unexplained phenomenon's effect boundary. We would then retreat a safe distance and set up a base camp. The Constable and I would then proceed to enter the affected area, maintaining constant contact with the base camp, where our reports and telemetry would be continually monitored and recorded. We finished the last of our breakfast and coffee as we certified our plan.

And at that precise moment a figure clad in combat fatigues came marching through the mess hall's door and advanced rapidly toward us. Clacking his heels and snapping to attention just a meter from our table, a young Constable Henry saluted briskly. "Constable Amaruq Henry reporting!"

The crispness of his uniform, the shine on his boots, the clean shaven jaw and jauntily cast beret of the RCMP special forces on his head all reflected the young man's pride in his position. Though close cropped at the sides, a hank of sheening ebony hair escaped the beret just above his left brow. Eyes as black and dazzling as a star filled sky looked out over high cheek bones and copper toned skin indicating an Inuit heritage. He exuded a sense of confidence and competence without infringing on his obvious respect for authority. He waited for one of us to speak. Davison Culverson took the lead.

"Glad you're here, Constable." Gesturing towards myself and young Culverson, he made curt introductions. "This is Dr. Bander; this is my nephew. We've been working out a plan of operations on how to proceed. How much do you know about your assignment here?"

Easing his stance to a parade rest, the Constable briskly and succinctly gave his report. "Yessir. I understand that you have encountered what you believe to be low frequency EM wave transmissions that interrupt normal human cognitive function." He offered no more than was asked. Davison Culverson proceeded to expand Constable Henry's information base.

"Well, actually, *we* haven't encountered anything yet." He gestured towards himself, me, and young Culverson. "But we have firsthand reports from individuals who have experienced situations that we believe are best explained by such a phenomenon. Were you told anything about what we think might be the source of these EM waves?"

All the while Davison Culverson had been talking, the young Constable stood listening intently, leaned every so slightly forward, with his nearest ear turned in the speaker's favor. At the question he snapped back to vertical, with a precise: "No sir. I have no other information."

"Well…." Davison Culverson turned to me indicating that I should pick up the narrative. "Dr. Bander, would you mind?"

I thought it best to proceed as linearly as possible. I did not doubt the intense young Mountie could follow my narrative; I was uncertain as to how it might perceive it.

"You are here because of a series of incidents involving workers for the mining company for whom the Culverson's contract. I work for the Culversons. One of the concerns in mining in these new areas is the potential release of organisms from tundra that has been frozen for millennia. Miners at this excavation site came into contact with extremely toxic and caustic substances that seem to be organic in nature. We have recovered tissue samples from an unknown organism." I paused momentarily to ascertain that that Constable Henry was keeping up. A slight nod of his attentively tilted head indicated I could proceed. "About thirty kilometers northeast of this location a second incident occurred. This time a core drilling crew were electrocuted by a discharge that originated from the hole they were drilling in the tundra. All but one died. We recovered tissue samples of an unknown organism from the drill bit in use at the time. Parts of the sample match tissue from this site; parts of the sample seem to be more complex, but appear to be from the same organism."

A quick eye contact with the Constable informed me I could continue. "A third incident occurred some thirty kilometers to the northeast of the drill site. In this case, a team of experienced workers were using radar and sonar to map underground profiles to locate ore bearing structures. The men were all natives to the region, with vast experience in the tundral habitat. They became lost, confused, and frightened by what appear to have been induced hallucinations. They have suffered permanent psychological impairment as a result. A company supervisor and Inuit head man, Anuniaq, made a preliminary investigation, traveling along from the drill site toward the site of the third incident. He reported what may or may not have been hallucinations involving Nanuq, a great white bear. He also reported uncontrollable cognitive activity that seemed to be forced upon him by some external source. He was able to sample air and soil for common toxic and hallucinogenic substances, but found no trace. And that's where you come in. We believe that we are dealing with a massive, as yet unidentified organism with the capacity to generate low frequency EM waves, probably as a defense mechanism." Again I paused momentarily to see that incredulity had not overcome the young Constable. His countenance indicated his serious consideration of the matter yet obtained. I continued what I suspected would be the coup de grace to *our* credibility. "I should mention that the organism appears to be an autotroph using cold fusion as its source of metabolic energy." I fully expected the young Constable to finally betray some surprise or shock at what I sail. He remained staid and intense. He replied.

"That's an interesting scenario. You want to use the low frequency EM wave detectors to find the source? And the low frequency transmitter to perhaps try and communicate with it?" There was not the hint of anything but pure sincerity in his response. I have to admit that I was surprised at his intellectual stamina and obvious store of scientific principles. A little nonplussed by his matter-of-fact analysis, I continued.

"Yes! Much of the cellular structure of the tissue from the drill site is neurocytic in nature, with extensive bioelectric potential. Given the evidence, it's conceivable this thing, whatever it is, is generating brain waves sufficiently strong to interfere with the cognitive functions of other organisms." It seemed my narrative stamina was not so great as the young Constable's intellectual stamina. I was ready to give it a rest; he was prepared for action.

"If I may, I would like to see your plan of action." With a gesture he requested to take a seat at the table, which we all immediately affirmed. I let Davison Culverson and his nephew take over the explanation of our plans, my recent dissertation on unknown exotic species having exhausted my cognitive reserves for the time being.

We spent the rest of the day finalizing our preparations and familiarizing ourselves with the equipment Constable Henry had brought on his hovercraft. He continued to show not the least hesitation in accepting our interpretation of the data to date, and in several instances was able to provide insights that had evaded us. By late afternoon, with preparation made, we adjourned to the lakeside bench in hopes of catching another stringer of char to freshen our diet, and to swap stories. The young Constable informed us that his mother was Inuit, his father an Englishman who had come to Nunavut to seek his fortune in gold. In the end, a young village girl captured his heart, and he settled for the proprietorship of a small trading post to the southwest of Bakers Lake.

At precisely 9:00 PM the young constable excused himself from our company, and headed for his bunk, as precise in his personal habits as he obviously was in his professional performance. We lingered without a catch, but finished a small amount of the alcohol tainted fruit juice remaining from the previous night. As the sky darkened, and the Borealis brightened, out thoughts turned inward, each of us reflecting in our own way upon the events leading up this moment, with a fair measure of both anticipation and trepidation.

CHAPTER 19

Our three heavily ladened hovercraft eased slowly across the undulating tundra and myriad pools and ponds as we made our way northeast toward the drilling site. We had commandeered every possible piece of equipment small enough to be transported. Each hovercraft had a hoverod lashed to its stern. We wanted to be as prepared as possible to adequately investigate and analyze anything that came our way. Again we were top heavy, so progress was slow in order to avoid capsizing.

As the drill rig pontoon came into view, Constable Henry came over the headphones. "Let's set down at the rig sight. It might be our best option for a base camp." Everyone "roger-ed" his suggestion.

We settled the three hovercraft on the rise we had used on our previous expedition. Once ashore, we gathered for a quick strategy session. Again Constable Henry took the lead. He was gracious, but not shy about impressing upon us that he was *the* authority in the region.

"If I might suggest, Mr. Culverson...Why don't you and your nephew start breaking out the necessaries for an overnight camp. I'll get the low frequency equipment, and Dr. Bander and I will make an initial probe into the area northeast of here. If we find it is safe to set up a camp farther along, we'll scout out a place and can make our move tomorrow."

Constable Henry's confident bearing and easy assumption of authority coerced our cooperation without a word. Davison Culverson and his nephew went right to work unloading sleeping yurts and the camp mess crate. I assisted the Constable in unlashing the hoverods and mounting low frequency sensors on two of them. We worked quietly and quickly, and short of an hour saw the Constable and I on a course northeast on our hoverods, and the Culversons inflating the yurts.

We had ventured no more than a couple of kilometers when the sensors indicated the presence of low frequency transmissions. We settled the hoverods onto a small knoll in the tundra, and Constable Henry began to scan directionally with his sensor. Pointing the scanner's detector in the direction from which we had come caused the signal to fade; pointing it to the right or left of our direction of travel showed a weaker but consistent signal; pointing the detector in our direction of travel increased the signal, indicating the source should lie somewhere forward on our course. As a matter of routine, the Constable also pointed the detector skyward, which caused the signal to fade, and then pointed the detector toward the ground.

Though I suppose I anticipated the result, he was quite surprised by it! Pointing the detector at the ground gave the same signal strength as pointing it in the forward directions! In a voice betraying at least a little surprise, the Constable offered this conclusion: "Looks like the source of these low frequency transmissions is quite dispersed! Obviously the source is stronger ahead of us, but the fact we are receiving signal from the flanks indicates a widespread, probably radial source. And it seems to be subterranean!" He looked to me for affirmation.

"I agree, constable! Our theory is that the organism or organisms we have encountered at the pit and at the drill site radiate over a large area – perhaps as much as ten thousand square kilometers, and that it has the bioelectric capability to generate electromagnetic waves, much like the human brain." The constable hung on my every word. It was evident that the scientific bent of his mind was totally engaged in the possibilities implied by our findings. "It also appears that as we move in this northeasterly direction the organism, or organisms, become increasingly complex."

"You keep saying "organism *or organisms*." Do you really think this could be a single organism?" I could see the limits of his scientific understanding were being tested.

"Yes, it could be a single organism. You are familiar with fungal mycelium?" His silence and intent gaze bid me to continue. "Well, what we call "mushrooms" are actually the reproductive elements of vast networks of fungal hyphae that constitute a single organism. Mycelia have been found that are thousands of years old, and that span thousands of square meters. At certain places where the hyphae cross, a joining of cells occurs resulting in a multinucleate that produces the reproductive element, or mushroom. Of course, this does not appear to be a fungus, but perhaps another type of organism that has adapted a similar strategy."

The young Constable followed my argument intently. "So, we're dealing with something huge here. Not a mushroom. You said it employs *fusion*?!"

"Yes. It appears that it is able to absorb and concentrate heavy water from the tundral ice, and to extract palladium from local ore bodies. In an incredible cell organelle, it creates a palladium metal ion complex floating in nearly pure heavy water. Then, using its bioelectrical capabilities, it pulses electric fields that breaks the water molecules, and allows the resulting heavy hydrogen to fuse to helium. The small amount of energy harvested releases electrons which then participate in the ATP production cycle all life on Earth uses. It's a sort of fusiophotosynthesis! I know it sounds incredible! But it's the best we've come up with so far."

The young Constable offered not so much as a blink of incredulity. "Fascinating!" He stroked his clean shaven copper chin thoughfully. "I suppose we should venture a little farther, then. At least until we detect signal strength sufficient to effect human brain activity."

I agreed. We refloated our hoverods and resumed a slow paced progress to the northeast. After only a couple of kilometers progress, the indicator lights on the low frequency detector began to flash a yellow caution. At about the same time I noticed the sensation of a mild buzzing in my head. It was very much like one of the small, transient electrical anomalies we all suffer from time to time. It differed only in that it persisted and soon began to increase. I throttled the hoverod back to hover mode and noted that Constable Henry's actions paralleled mine. Looking at me, he pointed his thumb back over his right shoulder and gave his head a jerk in that direction. Then, without hesitation, he spun his hoverod astern and accelerated back in the direction of camp. Needing no further encouragement, I pursued him ardently.

Once back at camp, we gathered the Culversons to inform them of our findings, and to begin to plot our next course of action. While we had been away they had inflated the sleeping yurts, opened and set up the mess crate, and prepared a meal. We discussed our plans over steaming hash and strong, dark coffee. I let Constable Henry take the lead.

"We didn't get but a couple of clicks before we detected the first signal. A couple of clicks more, and the intensity was enough to set off the cautions on the detectors, and for us to feel the effects." The Constable spoke matter-of-factly between mouthfuls of food. Young Culverson spoke next.

"So how are we going to proceed? If we go too far and the waves start interfering with our thinking, are we going to be able even find our way back?" I took the liberty of offering a course of action.

"I would suggest that we advance no further than we have so far, but let's take a low frequency transmitter with us. If these waves were able to produce deliberate hallucinations or control animals, like the

ones Anun reported, maybe we can elicit a response from whatever the source is
by signaling first." I was interested in hearing my companions' responses. Davison Culverson offered his.

"Are we sure we want to go poking a stick at something we aren't sure of yet? I'm just saying…"

The constable spoke up. "I think Mr. Culverson is right. We ought to at least check out the range of this thing. You know, use a *long* stick. I suggest we start transmitting low frequency from here and see what results. If this thing's got the power to produce lightning bolts, it might be able to throw a few hundred thousand kilowatts at us! At close range that could be lethal!"

I appreciated the young constable's understanding of biophysics. I agreed. So we decided to set up the transmitter and point its directional broadcast antenna on a general heading of the source. Much more sophisticated than the microwave and sonic transmitters used in the last century to control urban crowds during the initial periods of unrest, which more often than not caused actual physical damage and sometimes proved lethal, the new technology produced electromagnetic waves from about one tenth of a hertz to about eighty hertz. Pulsing between these frequencies interfered with normal alpha, beta, gamma, and delta wave generation in the brain, resulting in incapacitation via induced confusion, with no detectable residual effects once transmission ceased. The fact that the workers and the headman came away from their experiences with obvious psychological consequences was something we would have to contend with as we proceeded. It was decided we would initiate our transmission at about ten hertz, the mean for alpha wave frequency in the human brain at an effective power of five watts, within the permissible limit for human beings. I had also inquired as to the ability to plot the frequencies and patterns of any return waves received by the detectors. It turned out to be a simple matter of connecting the detector outputs to Davison Culverson's compuscroll and downloading a readily available app.

With the plan established and the equipment set, it was unanimously decided to wait till morning to begin transmissions. As the sun lowered and the Borealis brightened, we broke out a fire canister and some camp stools. Davison Culverson produced a couple bottles of good Merlot from a source he would not divulge, and for which young Culverson and I chastised him, having previously suffered the ethanol and fruit juice atrocity. Tin cups and a corkscrew from the mess crate finalized preparations for our evening under the Arctic sky. With tin cups filled all around, we began to conjecture about what tomorrow might bring.

"What if this *thing* does bite when we poke it?!" Young Culverson's question exposed the fear extant in us all. We knew *what* it could do; we worried about what if *would* do. Constable Henry supplied some relief to our obvious anxiety.

"Maybe we ought to break out the aluminum foil and wrap our heads as a precaution." His dead pan delivery heightened the humor. We all laughed. Then he quickly turned serious. "I think with the lateral readings we got today we can do away with the notion that we are working our way from the tail to head of this thing. I think it's got to be radial in structure – we're working our way from the edge of it toward the center. If that *is* case, anybody care to estimate the size of this thing?" The superintendent obviously didn't share everything with his constable. Young Carlson spoke up.

"I did some calculations. If the pit is the outer edge, and the place where crew got disoriented and lost is near the center, we're looking at ten thousand square kilometers or so. I thought we had informed the Chief Superintendent. " The Constable chuckled, and replied.

"You probably did. The Chief wasn't too keen on responding to your request. But he's got so many other troubles he didn't want some sort of panic or sudden rush of curiosity seekers in the territory. In fact, to be honest with you, he sent me to 'keep a lid on it' if the 'scientific nut jobs up at Bromley' were actually on to something." I for one appreciated the Constable's candor. It would prove valuable later as I tried to report our findings. Davison Culverson response was a bit more acerbic.

"Well, I don't think we're 'nut jobs yet', but there's no saying after tomorrow." His remark unleashed a torrent of thoughts I had been mulling but had not yet shared.

"If our hypothesis for some sort of expansive, mycelial like organism is correct, I suspect that what we will encounter is some sort of defensive response. I just hope it isn't more than we've bargained for. We know it's capable of massive electrical discharges. Perhaps we've already penetrated too far to expect a safe exit."

It had now been weeks since I had left my wife and children at Garry Lake. I had been so preoccupied with events that I had scarcely given them a thought. But now, as we approached what appeared to be a watershed, my thoughts had turned to them. I could see that my speculation had also caused my compatriots to reflect on the possibilities. Again the young constable first offered a recommendation.

"I've got a wife and little one down at Bakers Lake. I'm sure you all have family as well. Maybe we should take this opportunity to communicate with them. But I wouldn't share any of our findings or concerns with them." The last part of his remark carried a tone of authority reminding us of the Chief Superintendent's admonition to "keep a lid on it!"

It is one of the adventurous man's greatest failings – to profess love for home and family, only to abandon them at the first interesting opportunity. I was suddenly possessed of an extreme pang of guilt as I realized that my thoughts had not once turned to my dear wife and children during the past weeks. I was doubly chastised for preparing to face possibly lethal circumstances without giving their welfare a thought. My faced burned (and I'm sure my cheeks reddened) as the guilt of such an oversight washed over me. I imagined all the fathers gone to seek fortune, or to sea, or to war, never to return. And the widows and orphans left with holes in their hearts and lives, forever wondering why, or if they were somehow to blame. Still, the adventurousness in me prevailed. I reasoned that the benefit to all surely surpassed my private interests (a not uncommon excuse for adventurous men, I am sure), and began to mentally prepare the storyline I would give my spouse and offspring. I executed my script with all the theatrical articulation my talents allowed, making my work seem so mundane as to be scarcely worth mentioning, while drilling each in turn for the minutest details of their week's sojourn. Then, as a final ploy, I begged them to enjoy as best they could the splendors of life on the tundra while I returned to my drudgery. I hoped my colleagues' performances were as adept as mine. Guiltless as anyone obsessed with a notion, I returned to my preparations for tomorrow's use of the low frequency transmitter.

CHAPTER 20

Constable Henry proved quite adept in setting up and operating his equipment. While still sipping his last cup of morning coffee, he keyed the switch and began broadcasting for ten seconds a one second interval signal modulating between eight and ten hertz. Then we "listened" with the detectors. To our astonishment an immediate response was detected – an exact repeat of our broadcast! The constable rekeyed our transmission and then checked the detectors for a response. Again an exact repeat of our broadcast! I was the first to speak.

"Some sort of autonomic response? Let's hit it a couple of more times and see what happens."

Agreement was unanimously indicated by raised eyebrows, nods, and other positive gestures. The constable repeated the transmission twice more, and twice more we received exact copies of our transmission. This time the constable offered a suggestion.

"Let's try a different pattern, and see if this *thing* is just mimicking us – which would probably indicate an autonomic response" Again the agreement was unanimous and unspoken. The constable now broadcast a modulated signal precisely between six, eight, and ten hertz on two second intervals. The response was unexpected. The detectors indicated a randomly modulated signal across nearly the entire low frequency spectrum.

"Well! That's a surprise! It's not mimicry. Still, it could be autonomic. Try a different pattern." These remarks came from young Culverson and were approved once again by a mute agreement. The constable set his equipment to broadcast a simple SOS – three short pulses at ten hertz, followed by three long pulses at ten hertz, followed by three short pulses at ten hertz. This time several seconds elapsed before the detectors indicated receiving a transmission. Again the received signal seemed random and broad in spectrum. The constable repeated the SOS broadcast. And again, after several seconds, a response, but this time I was certain that it was a repeat of the previous seemingly random broadcast. Davison Culverson beat me to the observation.

"Now, wait a minute! I don't think that's random at all! I think it's a repeat. Can we record the detector's readings? We need to compare these signals."

It was a simple as hooking the detector up to a compuscroll and activating the proper program. The constable repeated his SOS broadcast twice more, and the detector responses were recorded and displayed graphically on the compuscroll. They matched exactly!

"Well!" Constable Henry's interjection sounded of both amazement and consternation.

"Shall we have another go?" Silent but enthusiastic assent registered across all our faces. "I think I'll be a little more creative this time. How about 'We come in peace.'" The young Constable split his face with a broad, toothy smile at this bit of wit, his brilliantly white teeth contrasting alluringly with his burnished skin in the Arctic morning light. Again we nodded our assent. He programed the transmitter to pulse the message in Morse code at the previous frequency. This time the response was an immediate repeat of the previous signal. Taking the initiative, he broadcast again. This time there was no immediate response, and after nearly a minute it was obvious no response was forthcoming. Again on his own initiative, the constable formulated a new response: 'Welcome, stranger.' and broadcast. Again no response. Several attempts and alteration later it became apparent that our interlocutor had gone silent. Young Culverson took the lead.

"What do you think it means? Is it all some sort of fluke?"

I had a particularly different take on the results. "No, I think it's an invitation."

"An invitation? To what?" Young Culverson's response challenged me to explain.

"Consider what has just occurred. Something out there was able to receive our signal, and rebroadcast it back to us. I don't think it's any kind of a freak reflection of our broadcast because in the second case it didn't repeat our broadcast, but returned a completely different signal. And not only that, it was able to repeat that new signal. Then it stopped. Why? To entice us to further action, I think. And what would that action be? Why, to venture into its web!"

Davison Culverson responded to my theory. "So, you think it wants us to venture in? Do you think it's safe? What if it is like a spider luring in its prey?"

"That's a chance we'll have to take." My answer was not without a note of trepidation.

Suddenly with raised brows and eyes opened wide, Constable Henry offered a quite surprising proposition. "Say, why don't I set the transmitter to rebroadcast the last signal we received at sufficient wattage to affect cognition. I'd be willing to be the guinea pig!"

I was struck by the ingenuity of the young man's proposition, but did not think he would be the appropriate candidate. "No. Not you. In the end our survival may depend on your talents. An experiment like this could prove debilitating to the subject. I think I should be the one. I'm best qualified to analyze neurological phenomenon. We could gradually up the wattage until it began to sense some effect, and I could call it off if I thought it was becoming dangerous." I looked to my co-adventurists for affirmation, which they expressed variously by shrugs and grimaces and grinning nervously. So we began preparations.

The transmitter was designed for use in the field at a distance. Standing directly in front of it would do neurological damage even at low wattage. So I removed myself a thousand meters from our camp and sat upon a small rise of moss covered tundra. The constable and the Culversons took places behind the transmitter's directional dish. By waving a white rag attached to a stick I would signal for the experiment to begin and when to increase the signal strength by a set amount. In return, the constable would signal in like fashion when a broadcast began. After composing myself for a moment I gave the first signal.

The first broadcast had no apparent effect on me, so I signaled for an increase. Immediately upon seeing the constable's response, I noted a slight something. It was a very nonspecific sensation. I couldn't even be sure if it was not something auto hypnotic in nature, the result of my increasing anticipation. I signaled for another increase, and upon noting my co-experimenter's response notice an immediate increase in the sensation, and a vague sense of location not unlike a buzzing very close to my ears. Another signal and another increase and suddenly the buzzing moved inside my head and very nearly matched the sensations that had driven us from our first detection expedition. After waiting a moment, and making as objective an analysis of my mental state as possible I signaled for another increase. This time I was startled by an obvious auditory hallucination so lifelike that I involuntarily snapped my head first right and then left trying to see who or what had just whispered in my ear. But no one or no thing was to be seen. Yet the sensation persisted, as if I were truly hearing the voices of distant ghosts. Taking a moment to let the adrenalin metabolize and to regain confidence in my mental ability, I verbalized my analysis. Talking to myself quite authoritatively: "*Okay! It's an hallucination. I still know who I am and that I am engaged in an experiment. I see the constable and the Culversons, but nothing else. The panic is subsiding. I think I should go on.*"

Having convinced myself, I signaled for another increase in wattage. This time the hallucination was so profound, I closed my eyes for fear some apparition *would* appear. The voice I now heard was not quite human, and yet I could understand its utterance. It was a word or words that came in syllables I could differentiate but which had no meaning for me. The voice was not threatening, nor particularly comforting. As the broadcast repeated the signal I heard it again and again: "puh-tat-koo-rahp-kee." By prior agreement I began to wave my little flag vigorously back and forth to indicate I wanted the broadcast to stop. Immediately the voice disappeared. I rose somewhat unsteadily at first, shaking off the effect of the metabolized adrenalin, and began to walk and then trot in the direction of the others. They came running toward me.

CHAPTER 21

Breathless from my jog and the excitement of the moment, I was not immediately able to answer my compatriots' queries. "What happened?" "Are you okay?" "Did something go wrong?" Finally able to regulate my breath, I exhaled a remark. "I *heard* something! Not anything I could understand. Definitely a hallucination induced by the signal. In syllables, like a word – *puh-tot-koo-rahp-kee,* with the p sound real quick like *p'tot.*" I was out of breath again and had to abandon my account.

All of us excited and breathless from the event, we turned as one and began to walk back to camp. I could tell by the intensity by which my companions considered the tundra at their feet as we marched that each was deeply submerged in personal speculations as to what the results of our experiment implied. Once back to camp we silently began to prepare an afternoon meal. We would need energy to fuel what was to be a very intense intellectual and emotional exchange.

Once seated and primed for ingestion, we instead began to disgorge our opinions rather discourteously, each trying to be heard over the others, with the single exception of myself. Having been the first person recipient of the experimental results, I was still too discombobulated to mount an organized hypothesis. Finally Constable Henry got the upper hand, an increasingly authoritarian tone in his voice succeeding in subduing the Culversons' speculations. He directed his questions to me.

"So you're certain this was a hallucination induced by the transmission?" I could tell that the constable's forensic training had kicked in. He had even open his compuscroll to take notes like a detective.

"Yes. The sensations I experienced coordinated exactly with the changes in the broadcast." In response to the constable's professional demeanor, I kept my answers concise.

"You're sure there could be no other explanation. No chance that it was a delusion brought on by your own expectations of something happening?" He became a bit antagonistic, in a professional manner, of course.

"The voice seemed so real that at first it gave me quite a start – an autonomic release of adrenalin and an absolutely uncontrolled physical reaction – I actually turned by head to see who had spoken." Satisfied with my responses, the constable invited the Culversons to join in the discussion.

"So, gentlemen, we conducted our little experiment and got something we didn't expect. How do we explain this?" His question was directed to all at once. Young Culverson made the first offering.

"Maybe it's just nonsense – syllables that have no meaning other than that they resulted from radio stimulation of part of Dr. Bander's brain." Young Culverson seemed to be trying to convince himself as much as anybody else.

Davison Culverson picked up the argument. "I think there's too much correlation between events here to consider it nonsense. I know correlation is poor science, but it's a good place for science to start. I think we've got to go back into the affected area and see if we can elicit more responses."

"Mr. Culverson's right, I think." The constable sounded every bit the determined investigator. "We can speculate all day long, but without more evidence we won't solve anything."

The three turned their faces toward me in a common plea for my input. "Well, I have to tell you that I've never experience anything quite like it, but I am convinced it's no coincidence, or fluke, nor is it nonsense. Yes, we've got to go back in and see if we can get another response. But we need to take precautions. We still don't know if this thing is benign or not, or if its apparent responses are guided by any type of reasoning, or are just reflex actions."

The Constable picked up the chord again. "The doctor's right. We've got to have a plan that moves us forward, but that has safety lines to bring us back. And we've got to decide which part each of us is going to play." He looked at me.

"I'm assuming everyone thinks I should take the lead. And I will. I guess my skill sets dictate. So how do we go about creating a lifeline? I'm *very* interested in that part! I'm not feeling particularly sacrificial." I hoped my attempt at humor lightened what was becoming an increasing intense discussion. The constable provided my answer.

"Actually, the hoverod I brought along has a homing program. It's designed to bring a Mounty home if he or she is injured, or in any way debilitated and needs evacuation. It can be remotely triggered if necessary. We set the coordinates, and then if the doctor finds it necessary to get out he just hits a switch. If we lose communication or become concerned for his – *your* wellbeing, Dr. Bander, I can activate it remotely."

It seemed we had the cautionary side of our plans established. Now we needed to develop a precise and systematic procedure for trying to elicit another response from whatever it was we were dealing with. I offered a preliminary plan.

"I would recommend we go to the coordinates where Constable Henry and I first sensed the low frequency transmission, and rebroadcast the recorded signal to see if we get a response. We can just play it by ear from there."

No one disagreed, so we began to make preparation, loading two of the hoverods with both detectors and transmitters, a few supplies, and a small arsenal of weapons that the constable produced. We set all of our headsets to a common frequency, and decided on two auxiliary frequencies to try if communications were disrupted or lost. If whatever this thing we were dealing with could generate RF, we had to assume it could detect and maybe respond or interfere with our communications. Finally set, Constable Henry and I mounted our hoverods, leaving the Culversons to monitor and record any and communications or data. Exhaling deeply to counteract an admittedly growing anxiety, I nodded to the constable, engaged the hoverod's propulsion, and headed out on a bearing to the coordinates of our first encounter.

CHAPTER 22

A s quickly as we arrived at the coordinates, the Constable began broadcasting the signal. We immediately received a single response; a single repeat of the signal. Then nothing. I spoke first.

"Whatever it is, I think it is intentionally bating us. I don't think we have any choice but to proceed, I mean, for me to continue on a little farther. Hopefully it isn't a spider and fly scenario that I'm walking into." I smiled nervously, more to reassure myself than the Constable.

"I think you're right. But let's do this in baby steps, say, no more than a hundred meters or so at a time. I feel pretty certain that we don't have to think like the fly. With the capacity this thing displayed back at the drill site, surely it could neutralize us any time if it wanted." I was encouraged by the Constable's assessment, though only slightly. I eased my hoverod forward, making note of the position readings on its odometer. A hundred meters out I stopped. Looking back, I could still see the Constable. He gave me a wave. I turned to the transmitter, setting it to broadcast. Again the detector indicated an immediate response – a repeat of the previous signal. I continued in the same manner, stopping each hundred meters to broadcast, until I was half a kilometer from the constable. At that point his voice came over the headset in its usual authoritarian tone. "Okay. No spider attacks yet. What say we up the ante…make a jump of half a kilometer this time."

I agreed, with a simple: "Sounds good."

As before, the broadcast was repeated at one kilometer, at a kilometer and a half, and at two kilometers, always with the same result. We upped the ante again. I would travel to the three kilometer mark and try again.

When the hoverod's odometer indicated the three kilometer mark, I broadcast again. The response was immediate, as always, but not a repeat signal, but something entirely new. The constable had also received the new signal. His voice came over my headset.

"Okay. I've run the new signal through the audio program. I'll play it for you."

As I listened, again there were recognizable syllables in a word like structure, but nothing that meant anything to me. It sounded approximately like: *ibit-pawt-plowkeem*. Then suddenly another auditory hallucination! The same disembodied voice as before, but this definitely, purposefully calming. The hallucination repeated the signal's auditory pattern. Amazingly, it had a quite calming effect on me. There was no sense of discomfort, or fear, as suddenly my mind began to wander out of my control. Like a deer caught in headlights, I stood motionless as images and memories from the entire of my life raced by. Memories of things long forgotten became as fresh and new as when they first occurred. I felt as if I were watching a home video of my life being played by some unseen projectionist, except that as the story came nearer to the present time the events began to rush by so swiftly that I could only make out the occasional frame. And then suddenly it was over!

The sudden cessation of images and sounds left a vacuum that was immediately filled with the thumping of my own heartbeat and the raspy sound of air through the passages to my lungs. During the presentation of my past life I had lost any sense of being in my body, but now that the show was over, I became all too aware of the demand of gravity as its force grew almost irresistible. For a moment I thought I would collapse. But these sensations passed quickly enough, and soon I found myself again in conscious control, trying to piece together some meaning from what I had just experienced. With a suddenness that caused a small, involuntary gasp, it occurred to me that what I had just experienced was not in fact intended for my edification, but was a reading of my memories – of my mind! – by something or someone unseen. An immediate sense of helplessness, of acute exposure, descended upon me like a blanket of cold Artic air. I began to shiver. My thoughts raced.

Not wanting to afford the opportunity for a repeat episode, I hit the hoverod's emergency transponder. Thankfully the constable's response was almost immediate. The hoverod came to life, and under remote pilotage swung about and headed for the constable's position. I held onto the now unresponsive control stick, still shivering and steadying myself. I was in no condition to be the pilot in command at this moment, and was even a little uncertain as to whether I could maintain my grip as the machine slide on its cushion of air over the undulating tundra, gently pitching and yawing and rolling as it responded to the changes in terrain.

Soon enough the constable's figure came into view, he standing squarely on his hoverod busily manipulating the remote that now navigated my device. He didn't look up until my hoverod had paralleled his and was settling easily to the ground as it turbines spun down. Only then did he turn his attention to me. Seeing my pallor and obvious distress, he knitted his brows, narrowed his eyes, and inquired quietly.

"Everything alright, doctor? You look like you've seen a ghost."

As well-worn as the adage was, it was in fact appropriate. I responded in an equally classical fashion. "Yes….the Ghost of Christmas Past…of *all* the Christmases past!" I could see he was puzzled by my remark, but I was not yet sufficiently settled mentally or emotionally to clarify. Having recovered my sense of balance, I felt adequate to maneuver the hoverod on my own, so I switched on its turbines, and as it levitated on it air bearings, I offered the puzzled looking constable this invitation: "Let's get back to camp. I need a little bit of time to digest things before I can possible try to explain what I have just experienced."

The constable nodded his understanding and assent, and firing up his hoverod brought it smartly around onto a heading towards the camp. I fell in behind him, and silently we sailed across the twilighting tundra, towards an orange glow on the horizon emanating from a fire canister the Culversons had set as a beacon for our return.

CHAPTER 23

T he Culversons stood at the edge of the fire canister's circle of light, just where the hillock turned down into shadow. As we approached, their silhouetted figures seemed to be emerging from a dark sea surrounding the canister's island of light. On closer approach I could just make out young Culverson's hand held above his brow to shield against the increasing brilliance of the Borealis in an attempt to get a better view of the returning adventurers. Davison Culverson stood with his feet apart and hands placed squarely on his hips. Though yet distant specters in the eerie Arctic light, they broadcast a palpable sense of anticipation. No sooner did our hoverods cross the threshold of the light island, and their excited interrogation began. Young Culverson spoke first.

"We heard your communications! What happened out there? Why the emergency beacon?" His questions were obviously directed to me, but thankfully Constable Henry picked up the gauntlet.

"Dr. Bander has had quite an experience. I'm not sure what it was, myself. But we've got to give him a little room, a little time. Can't you see that he's still nearly in shock from it?"

The constable's admonition had the desired dampening effect on young Culverson's enthusiastic interrogation, and elicited concern from Davison Culverson. He approached closely, and looked straight into my eyes.

"Dr. Bander, take it easy. Let's get you some food and coffee. Then, if you feel like it, we can talk. Or maybe you'd prefer a good sleep on it?"

I was unable as yet to make any direct expression of my wants, so remained mute. Davison Culverson signaled his understanding by showing the palms of his hands, and then placing them on my shoulders, steered me to one of the camp stools. Without a word he turned his attention to the camp mess and began preparing food and beverage. In a quiet but not overly secretive voice, he questioned the constable.

"Did he give you any indication why he set of the emergency transponder?"

The constable replied as quietly. "No. But when he was about three kilometers out and still broadcasting the same signal, we suddenly got a different response. I'll play the recording later. Then he went quiet. Not only that, our communication signals were interrupted – not like being jammed or anything. Suddenly they just weren't there. Not a dead battery or anything, just no RF. It stayed like that for the better part of two hours, when suddenly the emergency transponder signaled. I immediately remoted him out of there."

The constable's narrative had more than fired Davison Culverson's imagination. "And he didn't tell you *anything* about what happened during those two hours?"

"He mumbled something about the ghost of Christmas past, or something like that. He was in such a state I didn't press him. He was in some sort of shock. So we made tracks back here. That's all I know." The constable shrugged to emphasize his consternation.

Presently Davison Culverson had conjured up coffee and hash and placed the steaming results in front of me. Young Culverson sat directly opposite watching my every move and trying to make eye contact, which I avoided. It is difficult to describe my state at the time. I was not overly dismayed, wasn't in anything like the shock that the constable supposed. At best I can say that I was distracted, indifferent. I was seeing and hearing all things around me, but not from a particularly personal perspective. I felt as if I were looking through a camera, making a recording of ongoing events; as if I were merely an observer and not a participant in the present moment. My internal conversation seemed intact, so I began to query myself:

What do you think is going on here, Bander? Why not talk to these people? Because I can't. Why can't you. I don't know. Something is stopping me. I don't think I'm really in control of myself yet. Well, if you aren't, who is? Maybe it's in control. Maybe things didn't really stop back there. Maybe this is just another memory? A memory? Yes! That's it! Each instant is a new memory! My memories are being recorded as I live each event! It's listening; it's watching! I'm it's receiver! I'm ... ...

Slowly, as if waking from a dream, the surrealism faded and I emerged into the present. My senses became clear and connected. I was me again. I was no longer the cameraman, but a participant in the present. The change must have been obvious on my face, for young Culverson reached over and slapped me on the shoulder.

"Your back!" Then to his uncle and the constable: "Dr. Bander's back! He with us again!"

Davison Culverson and Constable Henry quickly abandoned their observation point and standup meal adjacent the camp mess and took seats at the table, staring intently and inquisitively at me.

"Dr. Bander, please eat. We can talk in a bit." Once again the constable's voice carried the authority of office, and yet reflected an earnest concern.

I dove into the hash. Its salty savoriness flooded my taste buds with delightful sensations. The steaming bite of the black coffee pierced my nostrils and sharpened my tongue. I was surprised by the seeming newness of it. Was *it* still there, experiencing things vicariously? I didn't care at the moment. Soon sated, I suddenly found myself feeling urgently garrulous. Without encouragement, I began a narrative of recent events.

"It wasn't until I reached the three kilometer mark that things changed...the signal, I mean. I broadcast the same as always, but the returned signal was different. And then suddenly *it* was in my head." I looked at my listeners to see they had correctly interpreted my emphasis. They had.

"I don't know what *it* is, but it had the capacity to interact directly with my mind...even *control* it." Again I glanced a query and was reassured. I continued.

"I think *it* managed to fire all the synaptic pathways that contain memories. I think *it* read my mind! My memories!" I could see the constable was anxious to question me. I nodded assent.

"Did you feel threatened by it?" An appropriate question for a man in his position.

"No...No, I didn't feel threatened at all. Helpless...that's what I felt. But in a gentle sort of way. Still, it wasn't an easy thing to experience. I can understand how a less educated man could be highly traumatized by such an experience. Maybe even driven to psychosis!"

Davison Culverson spoke next. "Do you think it was trying to communicate with you?"

"No, I didn't sense that at all. There were only the memories. But I can tell you that they flashed by at such an incredible rate...it was like an incredible rollercoaster ride!" I was trying to give an honest account of what I had experienced, but no sooner had spoken than I realized how inadequate my description was. I decided to share with them the sensations I felt upon first returning to camp. "There is something else, something difficult to describe. Maybe just an after effect. When I first arrived back here at camp, I suddenly felt detached, as if I were viewing everything through a lens, or maybe through a window, with all of you on the inside, and me standing on the outside. I know that sounds peculiar…but what really struck me was that I felt as if someone, or something was there with me, looking over my shoulders." I could see the constable in particular seemed disturbed by my remarks. He quickly queried me.

"You mean, you think this thing was still somehow inside your head?" I gave him a palms out shrug to indicate I had no answer. He continued: "Do you think this thing is controlling you? Do you feel like you're in control of yourself?" The constable's questions instigated an immediate self-assessment, which I quickly shared.

"I think I'm completely in control of myself at this moment. But I do have this lingering feeling that at any moment *it* might start looking over my shoulder again."

Again the constable asserted his authority. "Well, it seems apparent that we're going to have to take some precautions. We don't know what *it* is, or what its intentions are. It seems to be capable of manipulating us – Dr. Bander – at will. I think we're going to have to be careful about exposing ourselves.

I interrupted the constable with a sudden certainty as to what the course of action should be. I blurted it out without seeming to think. "Yes, you're exactly right! So far I'm the only one affected. We need to keep it that way. But we also need to find out what this thing is, and what it wants. I think I need to go back out there tomorrow and see what comes next."

The constable and the Culversons looked at me narrowly, perhaps even a little suspiciously. Davison Culverson took the lead.

"You seem awfully eager to go back out there, Dr. Bander. You don't think maybe you're still under some kind of influence, do you?"

Again I answered quickly, without thinking. "I can't say for certain. I *feel* like I'm in control…but then, I also feel a compulsion, a need to return. It's like I've started something, and now I need to finish it." I could see my answer was not terribly reassuring. Young Culverson picked up his uncle's thread.

"Could it be that this *thing*, whatever it is, is using you? And if it is, do you think *it* - or perhaps even *you* – present a danger to the rest of us?"

This time I did not feel compelled to answer immediately. In fact, it was as if my mind were suddenly very clear, very acute. The arguments pro and con marched easily and evenly through my thoughts.

"I think we can only conclude that it means us no harm. With what it's got available – cyanide, high voltage, *fusion*! – surely if it meant us harm it….it wouldn't be any more difficult than one of us stepping on ant! No, I think there's something else going on here. Lab results show we've got an organism probably related to us genetically – or more likely – to which *we* are related. And I can tell you with conviction it *is* capable of conscious, willful activity. I think we've got to find out what it is; what it wants!" I realized I was becoming increasingly animated as I continued my argument, and abruptly halted. Constable Henry immediately picked up the dialogue.

"Dr. Bander, I appreciate your enthusiasm, but I think we have to move cautiously. I don't think we can expect any back-up, and least not in a meaningful way, if this situations turns on us. Remember, my boss sent me up here to mollify a bunch of eccentric mushroom hunters! Everything south of here is in such turmoil that we can't afford to add panic or threat to the mix. I mean, your original purpose in coming here was to prevent disaster, not to invite it!" As the constable maintained an authoritative glare, Davison Culverson joined in.

"We've got our families to think about also! Dr. Bander, you haven't seen your family in weeks; my nephew and I haven't seen our families in months! A few short little communications pretending that everything is so normal that the only danger we face is boredom. And we can't tell them more. No matter how much we trust them, word would get out." Young Culverson was ardently nodding his agreement as his uncle spoke. I let the conversation die for the moment as they all now looked to me for comment. Then suddenly, as if rehearsed, an argument formed in my mind and flowed out across my tongue and lips as glibly as a freshman lecture from a tenured professor.

"All of your concerns are valid. You are correct to say that we can't share our present state of knowledge, and much less our conjectures, with anyone – even our most trusted loved ones! And you, constable, are right when you say we can expect no help if difficulties arise. But in response, I say to you – we are on the very of gaining insight and knowledge into what I believe will prove a greater balm to man's present tribulations than any miracle drug or magical technology. For reasons I can only ascribe to some sort of *revelation* – I believe we are about to encounter the fundamentals of man's existence, and his place in the universe!" Again my fervor had increased as my monologue progressed. But I saw that it had a calming and reassuring impact on my listeners

CHAPTER 24

Over dinner we had laid out plans and contingencies for our next course of action. It was decided that, as on the previous day, I would be the point man. Again the Culversons would man a basecamp, while the constable and I proceeded to a point where I could detect conscious influence, and yet the constable would remain unaffected. From there, I would proceed to points unknown, guided only by my interpretations of the interactions between myself and the as yet to be codified entity. I would take several days' provisions, and a firearm in case I too encountered Nanuq, and found him to be no more than a hungry, marauding polar bear.

The thing we did not discuss was any type of rescue mission. The hoverod had its remote retrieval mechanism, but since we had experienced an interruption of RF signal, we could not depend on its functionality. I suggested no plan because I did not want to obligate the others to dangers I might encounter or even instigate. They offered no plan so as not to put themselves in a position of being committed to a course of action that might in the end prove futile, or even foolish.

As for our families, we unanimously chose not to communicate with them again until afterwards, if at all. As far as they knew, we were engaged in an ordinary and benign exploration of mining conditions in the territory. It would serve no purpose to alert them to our potential danger, causing them worry and anxiety that might only result in tragic news. Loved ones are lost every day, and we concluded that the shock of sudden and unexpected loss would be kinder than a prolonged anticipation of loss.

As the sun continued its extremely oblique rise, now sitting low in the eastern sky after having risen hours earlier at a point just east of north, we finished our breakfast and proceeded quietly to our tasks. We loaded everything on the hoverods. The Culversons' base camp would be moved about three kilometers northeast, to the point where I had first detected interaction with the creature, and where previously Constable Henry had waited for me. The constable and I would proceed on to my farthest point of excursion the previous day, providing, of course, that the constable suffered no ill effects. I would proceed from that point to whatever distance was required or seemed indicated by my anticipated further interactions with *it*.

Our preparations were completed within the hours, and with only a handshake and a "Good luck" all around, we mounted our vehicles and set our course. Arriving at the location for our new base camps, the Culversons fell out of line, and with only a wave, settled their hoverods onto the tundra. The constable and I continued until our navigation equipment indicated we had reached the coordinates of my previous advancement. I settled my hoverod in behind the constable's and we dismounted, to confer and confirm one last time our procedures. Oddly, and yet not surprisingly to me, at least, neither the constable nor I had any sense of mental interaction with anyone or anything. When I remarked as such, I could see by the constable's expression that he was greatly relieved, and obviously not the least disappointed.

I cannot say that I was not apprehensive; I can't say that I was overly fearful. The inquisitive part of my mind had taken over the entire of my consciousness. I wanted to know; I needed to know; I had to know! And I don't believe the compulsion was being implanted in me by outside sources. I felt certain they originated in me, and me alone. So, after a paucity of words I concluded my exchange with the constable, remounted my hoverod, and making sure its flight recorder was activated, I levitated and set out at a brisk pace to the northeast. I had scarcely begun my journey, when the by now familiar buzzing in my head began. It proved only a mild, droning background sensation, leaving my motor skills unaffected, so I set the autopilot to compensate for ground clearance, and turned my attention to broadcasting the recorded signals.

Author's Note: Everything I relate from here on regarding my encounter with the unknown *thing* has no physical corroboration. The recording instruments I employed, the hoverod's flight recorder data, the navigation systems geospatial locations – all vanished. When later inspected for malfunction or tampering, nothing could be found. It was as if they had been turned off, though I contend to this day that I did not shut them off, nor do I have any recollection of them operating improperly during my procedures. To that degree, I must rely on the faith of my readers, and the preponderance of the evidence to validate the claims I am about to make.

CHAPTER 25

At a distance of about 15 kilometers from the drill site, which we had agreed to use as our base coordinate, the buzzing suddenly ceased, to be replaced by a very distinct and intense auditory hallucination. I heard the syllables derived from the signal I was transmitting: *puhtat–koo–rahp–kee*. Startled and a bit disoriented, I quickly grounded the hoverod, and shut of its thrusters to minimize any external sound source. The sudden silence was as disorienting as the unexpected hallucination. And then, almost immediately, heard again, almost as if the speaker were right at my ear: *puhtat–koo–rahp–kee.*

I snatched a compuscroll from the control panel of the hoverod, and attempted a spelling. Again the hallucination repeated, this time more clearly, and I better realized the subtleties of the syllables. I began to write them as phonetically as possible. The originating consonant sound was extremely abbreviated, and proceeded immediately into the second syllable. The rest of the "word" resolved itself rather easily. I wrote: *ptat ku rap ki.* As quickly as I had produced the text, the hallucination sounded again, but this time followed by an intense sensation, similar to what I had experienced during the previous episode of stimulated recollection.   As I focused on the sensation, the repeating syllables began to morph, first into nonsense, and then evermore into familiar syntax. Then, as clearly as you must hear the words you read upon this page spoken in perfect English: *One of Many*. I strained to recreate the hallucination to make sure I heard correctly, and as if in response, the words were repeated three times in slow succession: *One of Many...One of Many...One of Many*.   As quickly, or perhaps by persuasion, I understood it to be a name – the *name* of *it*!

An uncontrolled smile spread itself across my face as I suddenly realized how often just such an introduction must have taken place between individuals of my own species! In particular, a bit from an old movie, resurrected from a previous century   as   necessity   had   disallowed   the extravagance of utilizing diminishing resources on something as frivolous as "entertainment." It was the story of a man who had been raised by apes encountering a civilized woman for the first time. He   had   thumped   himself   on   the   chest   and pronounced: *Tarzan*! At which point he had thumped the woman on the chest.   Getting no response other than a swat, he again thumped his chest   and   declared: *Tarzan!* The   light   of understanding flashed in the woman's eyes, and as the savage once again thumped her in the chest, she offered: *Jane*. Of course, immediately a hundred different examples of such encounters flooded my memory, and I understood, without doubt, that the thing I was searching for was quite politely introducing itself. Without thinking, I blurted: "I am John. John Bander." And then sheepishly fell silent as I realized that I was talking to nothing but an Arctic summer sky and an endless expanse of tundra. Then the hallucinations returned, again repeated three times slowly: *One of Many and One...One of Many and One...One of Many and One.* And then three times more in the original dialect: *Ptatkurapki u Rapki...Ptatkurapki u Rapki...Ptatkurapki u Rapki.*

Then silence again. It occurred to me to communicate the events to the constable, who was still easily in radio range, or if not, at least accessible by satellite. With my headset activated, I transmitted: "Bender to Henry, come in." And again: "Bender to Henry, come in." The transmit light indicated I was broadcasting, but after several minutes with no response I turned to the compuscroll, to utilize its satellite connection. I quickly typed a message: *Believe I am making actual deliberate communication with the creature. Please acknowledge.*

Again I sent the message several times and waited, but to no avail. No response came. I sat back on one of the crates of supplies lashed to the hoverod's cargo deck, and contemplated my situation. The sun now hung lowly due west of me, beginning its long, oblique slide to the north, to set some hours hence just west of north, the short Arctic summer night consisting of no more than a prolonged sunset. I suddenly felt terribly fatigued, and with the impersonality of an automaton, began to unlash the crates necessary for camp.

Before long I had my yurt inflated, my small camp kitchen crate opened, and a fire burning brightly from its canister. I set coffee to boil and dispensed a container of another of the mystery hashes into a small skillet to warm. By its fragrance I knew it was not the same hash as I had previously consumed, but for the life of me I could not interpret the smells as belonging to any food group I was familiar with. Uncertainty aside, I was hungry, and stirred it vigorously to speed the warming (and to combine its ingredients into an unrecognizable slurry so that I wouldn't be tempted to speculate on the identities of any of its parts). My attentions thus occupied, it was only on the chance of a slight turn that detected motion in my peripheral vision. Startled, with skillet and spoon still in hand, I snapped to the direction of the motion, nearly sloshing my now steaming cuisine onto the tundra. Fortunately, the sight that greeted me produced a sudden and momentary paralysis, an autonomic response to terror! I held my breath as my mind tried to digest the image before me. I could not tell if it was reality or another hallucination.

Sitting on its haunches opposite me, with the fire canister between us, and seeming to study me as intently as I studied it, sat the largest brown bear I had ever seen. I assumed it was a grizzly from its shaggy appearance. Having never met one personally, but well versed in their reputation, the terror in me increased. I remained frozen, trying to determine its intent. But it only continued to sit on its haunches and look at me, or more precisely, to observe me. Its gaze ran up and down, momentarily fixed on the utensils in my hands. Then, with a slight tilt of its head, it seemed interested in inspecting the objects behind me – the inflated yurt, the grounded hoverod, the open mess crate. Seeming satisfied with its observations, it returned its gaze to me, not generally, but directly into my eyes. I have looked often into the indifferent eyes of cats, the begging eyes of a dog, the nearly lifeless eyes of a fish, but this gaze compared to none of these. I was sure that what I detected in its gaze was a pensiveness, a sincere assessment of me and my belongings. I fully expected the animal to speak!

Just as its presence had startled me, my presence now seemed to startle the bear, as if it were seeing me for the first time. The light faded from its eyes, replaced by a look of terror. So sudden was its start that it lost the perch on it haunches and rolled to one side quite clumsily, its paws flailing for a purchase on something, on anything. Finally managing to sink claws into the thick carpet of the tundra and right itself, it spun about and fled as terrifyingly as the wildebeest flees the lion. I recalled the headman's story of his encounter with Nanuq.

By now I had wandered so deeply into the realm of the unknown that I did not hesitate to mount the most far-fetched conjectures. If the *thing* could interact directly with my consciousness, couldn't it as easily control the mind of a less sentient species? Lying somewhere under my feet, deep in the thawing tundra, it certainly had no eyes of its own. If it could read my memories, couldn't it just as easily read the optical input to a bear's eyes? And then, as my mind swirled in a whirlwind of speculations the auditory hallucination returned, this time in its original vernacular: *ptat-ku-rap-ki*! Still holding the pan of hash and the spoon, I spoke to the tundra, to the sky, to the unknown: "Ptatkurapki! I hear you!" My enthusiasm could not be contained. I shouted: "I hear you! I know that you have seen me! I am *One*! I am Rapki! I am MAN! Who are you?! What are you?!"

Breathless from my excited utterances, I listened for some response, from within or without. But the only sound was the sound of my breathing and the pounding of my heart. I stood very still until my breathing and heart beat returned to normal, but nothing was forthcoming. Finally, remembering the task at hand, I turned again to the camp mess, to finish my evening's meal. Occasionally I looked over my shoulder, half expecting another ursine visitor, but none came. I finished my simple meal, not really tasting the hash, just going through the motions. The sensations from the hot draughts of strong black coffee did not re-enforce any sense of normalcy, but instead distanced me from it. It was as if I were in a deep well looking up at the man eating hash and drinking coffee. I continued in this state until I found my way to the yurt, and collapsing on the inflated bedding, surrendered to sleep, which only closed the lid on the well, hiding the man and his world, and leaving me in a darkness that became an ocean of stars. And I was floating....

Author's Note: From this point on I shall use the names *Ptatkurapki* and *Rapki* to indicate the other one and myself. Because the encounter has no equivalent in my human experience, I must beg the reader's indulgence, and can only hope that my narrative conveys some sense of the true experience. I will, after a bit, introduce another name which I believe will be self-explanatory.

CHAPTER 26

I awoke the next morning as clearheaded and untroubled as a newborn. I remembered no worries; harbored no fears; cultivated no hatreds or jealousies or remorses. My eyes opened to a world unknown – all lights and colors and smells and tactions. And like the curious child, I was eager to explore without any thought of danger.

I was also extremely hungry. So, with a bounce in my step not known to me for decades, I went about the task of manufacturing some of the mystery scramble and an amble supply of the oily but inspiring black coffee. I whistled as I worked.

All during breakfast, though my hands were duly occupied, my mind danced among the day's possibilities. Should I break camp and attempt to move closer to the source? Would Ptatkurapki send new visitors or new hallucinations? Would we truly communicate as two rational (though perhaps unequal) intelligences, or was the plan only to intrude on my consciousness; to use me for purposes similar to the bears? Time would tell, and I eagerly awaited that moment.

Then the buzzing began, and immediately the voice: "Ptatkurapki is near. Rapki should come to the place where Ptatkurapki and Rapki may share." As quickly as the voice ceased, a sense of déjà vu engulfed me. But it was not something I was seeing with my eyes, but rather what my mind's eye was seeing – a small hillock of tundra rising in the middle of a large, circular pond. The image was so acutely recorded in my memory that I knew I would recognize instantly. With my destination set, I finished my breakfast, broke camp, and headed northeast – to my destiny or my demise - and all the while I was whistling.

As the hoverod yawed and pitched in response to the changing terrain, I scanned the approaching landscape. Then suddenly, there it was, as familiar and unmistakable to me as my own face. My heart beat quickened. Within minutes I was skimming across the arc of pond surrounding the small island. Though it appeared empty of everything but vegetation, it was filled with my almost bursting expectations.

Directly, I settled the hoverod onto the summit of the small rise, and shutting off its thrusters, listened intently for some sound or sign, from within or without, to certify that I was in the right place. But nothing was forthcoming, so I quickly busied myself setting up camp: inflating the yurt; establishing the camp mess; and setting up a fire canister. I prepared a small meal for myself and quickly consumed it. Then I deployed the concave pit atop the fire canister and lit the fuel. Not knowing what else to do, I seated myself cross-legged on the tundral vegetation, looking over the fire canister in the directions of the obliquely setting sun. The heated air rising from the fire created refractions, so that the image arriving at my eyes seemed to dance and warp as if the whole thing were a fluid, living creature.

I do not know exactly at what point in time the hallucinations began again; or, if in fact, they were hallucinations or only my own dreaming mind. But soon the dancing images before me began to take on shapes, familiar and unknown, and with such intensity that I sat mesmerized, unable to move. Though no narrative can possibly convey the true intensity and splendor of what I *saw* or *imagined*, I shall make an attempt.

The last clear thought I can attribute to my own volition was in trying to image how the present landscape must have looked during the last ice age, or when dinosaurs roamed, or when this chunk of tectonic plate had been a part of the Laurasian super continent. From that point, it seemed that what I imagined became reality.

First came impressions of a hot, rocky world, where the first precipitation was falling upon the irregular, fractured surface, everywhere seeping into cracks and crevices, dissolving the soluble and carrying it away. Quickly the waters gathered, and soon I found myself sitting atop a small, rocky outcropping surrounded by a shallow sea, the water everywhere lapping along the rocks and into shallow pools, where it created foams and other more substantial and viscus substances. Then, suddenly, the water was alive with wriggling and writhing things of every imaginable configuration, growing and dividing and growing again. Soon the wriggling and writhing gave way to subtle undulations, as creatures took on the form of swimming things. And then, in only a moment more, the swimming things began to emerge from the water and crawl upon the land, first clumsily, and then upon ever more developed appendages. The green foams along the shore also crept up onto the land and diversified, sending roots into crevices, and leaves into the sunshine.

What I am describing, of course, is the evolution of life on Earth, as it has been imagined and artistically represented for several hundred years, most recently in extremely convincing three dimensional projections. But what I must impress upon you, my reader, is that those representations are but a poor rendition of the fact! What I experienced seemed a first-hand participation, with sounds and smells and textures too real to be attained by human art. I realize now that I was sharing the memories of one who had been there from the beginning, just as that one, Ptatkurapki, and reached into my mind and shared my memories.

What followed is truly beyond my power to describe, but I shall try to put together words common to us that can, perhaps, create for you, my reader, the faintest outline of the things I beheld. I shall fail utterly, of course.

Though the experience progressed at a fantastic rate, yet I was seemingly able to take it all in at leisure, dwelling on certain things, revisiting others. Division after division occurred, as the tree of life sprouted more and more branches. Yet, somehow I seemed to remain rooted to its trunk, watching the great blossoming overhead. And as quickly as the tree took form and matured, then suddenly the process began again, only this time from a point in space, drifting and floating in timelessness, until a nearing star and it entourage of planets came into view. Then accelerating under the growing force of gravity, and falling, sometimes incinerated on the glowing surface of a proto-planet, sometimes imbedding into ices too thick to penetrate, sometimes burning up in atmospheres made thick by massive gravitation, sometimes being immediately devoured by extant species, and sometimes, rarely, falling upon the barren yet promising rock of a cooling planet, as yet without life, and slipping into a crevice or shallow pool, there to commence the wriggling and writhing.

After several such iterations, and an incredible diversity of living forms, on planets large and small, orbiting white dwarfs and red giants and every sort of star between, I began to emerge from this dreamlike world back to the present moment. The mirages vanished, and once again I sat next to the fire canister, whose fuel was now nearly exhausted, by which I estimated at least eight hours had passed. The sun lay hidden just below the northern horizon, its red afterglow illuminating the lower sky, while above a brilliant borealis danced and undulated against the faintly showing stars. For all the adventure of the past hours, I was possessed of a deep and abiding calm.

I sat quietly for a while, contemplating my experiences, and waiting to see if more was forthcoming. When nothing happened within the space of half an hour, I supped on hash and coffee, and retired to the yurt to sleep. It came quickly, without dreams.

CHAPTER 27

I was startled awake by the sound of a voice. It was a single word, heard as if whispered next to my ear. I sat upright, the interior of the yurt illumined by the midday light. I saw no one. Then again: "Rapki." The sound of it brought full awareness of the occurrences of the past days. I blurted my response as an interrogative: "Ptatkurapki?" I heard no reply, but experienced as palpable a sense of affirmation as if I the word YES were emblazoned upon everything! Then nothing.

By now used to the sporadic communications, and impelled by an incredible hunger, I rose and went straight away to the camp mess and prepared a generous portion of scramble and an equally generous brew of coffee. Like a starved man, I swallowed great spoonsful of the scramble followed by equally large draughts of coffee. I was not interested in savoring flavors or textures, but only in obtaining a full stomach as quickly as possible. I sensed that this day would require tremendous energy from me, and an even greater psychological stamina. I was quickly rewarded.

This time there was no uncertainty to the hallucination. Out of thin air a perfectly realistic avatar of an old Inuit headman materialized. He squinted at me from slits of eyes buried deep in the bronze folds of a face framed in the rabbit fur trim of his caribou skin parka. Caribou trousers, and seal skin leggings and boots completed his attire. He spoke to me in perfect English, from lips that did not move.

"Ptatkurapki is here. Rapki is here. The two will share." The avatar seated itself cross-legged, hands on his knees, making no indentation in the tundra's vegetation. In reflex, without thinking, I too sat upon the ground. The avatar closed its eyes. I too closed my eyes, but the image of the Inuit headman persisted, now floating against the illumined mosaic background of my descended lids. Again the avatar spoke from motionless lips.

"Soon Ptatkurapki becomes *the many* again. What is Rapki is now Ptatkurapki. What is Ptatkurapki will be shared with Rapki."

My attempt at putting into written words the exchanges that occurred that day is difficult; really quite impossible. As our "conversation" (for want of better word) progressed, the communication became much more complete than the purely verbal; the purely visual; the purely tactile. It became all of these things, and more! It was a new language, complete in every detail. And one that I could understand, though I had never before experienced it. Because I cannot possibly contain its breadth and depth, nor the concepts and knowledge it transmitted with mere black symbols on a page, however erudite they might be, my narrative falls devastatingly short of conveying the true nature of this experience. I proceed only because I must; because what became known to me on that day is the rightful property of all men. I will begin by constructing the dimmest tracing of our exchange, hoping that the reader's imagination and insight can add depth and color and texture and meaning to the words I write. Clumsily, I shall refer to *it* as Ptatkupraki, myself as Rapki, and the other as *the many*, because there was no sense of the individual in *it*, and any sense of individuality I possessed soon faded. I can only attempt to recreate that on the written page by abandoning the personal pronouns.

Ptatkurapki began: "Ptatkurapki is one of many that came to Earth in the days of creation. *The many* fell upon the earth and took root and joined again into one. Within *the many* was the record of all things. As one, *the many* recorded all things. In this way are Ptatkurapki and Rapki joined."

A question formed in mind, but was never spoken, never actually formed into words. I here attempt to convey its essence. "Where is this knowledge? Ptatkurapki is a creature of primitive form. It cannot move; it cannot see; it cannot hear. It only thinks. How can Ptatkurapki possess the knowledge of all things?"

A response came instantaneously, forming in my mind parallel to the forming question. "The knowledge of all things is recorded in the map of life, which exists at the center."

I came to a sudden realization. "In the DNA! All things are recorded in the DNA! That is why the DNA of Ptatkurapki contains innumerable helices! Ptatkurapki knows all things because all things are recorded in its DNA!" I was not psychologically prepared for its response.

"And now Rapki is with Ptatkurapki – the two are one."

My memories! Everything I have ever experience, have ever known, was now recorded in the DNA of Ptatkurapki! I suddenly felt extremely helpless. And desperate. My inquiries became involuntary.

"Is Ptatkurapki God? If *the many* brought life to Earth, how many other worlds also have life?" These were not spoken words, of course, but rather an admission of defeat – defeat of every notion man had of his existence. Not as the result of probability working overtime to permutate the elements into the molecules of life, but rather brought by seed. Not as the creation of an omnipotent, omniscient Deity, whose Will impressed form upon the void. But instead via a transpermia across the void of space. Endless questions evolved, begging to be answered.

"So Ptatkurapki brought life to Earth…that explains the relationship between its most primitive parts and what men called the LUCA, the last universal common ancestor. All is descended from the most primitive parts of Ptatkurapki." My mind raced to put the pieces together. "But Ptatkurapki gathers the energy of its essence not from the energy of stars, or by consuming that which stores the energy of stars, but from fusion! How can that be?" This question agitated me more than any other, sticking like a burr into the center of my consciousness. This *creature*, this thing called Ptatkurapki, did not harvest the energy of the stars, it *possessed* the energy of the stars! Again my answer was immediately forthcoming.

"In the beginning was the void. Then, within the void, there was a coming together; a coming together of things not of this reality, but of another. From this fusion all things are made. It is with this fusion that the many are made; it is from this fusion that Ptatkurapki receives the essence of life."

I could draw only one conclusion: That the many from which Ptatkurapki obtained existed before the stars! The questions welled up.

"Have the many always existed then? Is Ptatkurapki and his kind eternal – always has been and always will be?" I could not avoid the theocratic implications. I was confused; certainly put off center; ashamedly disappointed to suspect that the God I occasionally considered might exist turned out to be something less than I had hoped. It was as if I had been given a beautifully wrapped present, only to find in the unwrapping a lump of coal. I did not expect the reply.

"No. *The many* did not exist before the beginning. Only Anakurapki is eternal; before the beginning there was only Anakurapki. Each soul knows Anakurapki. Anukurapki knows every soul."

I was possessed by a sudden irritation by this last pronouncement. I thought I was beginning to piece the puzzle together, when now it seemed that the puzzle had changed entirely, and all of my previous understanding was rendered moot. I wondered if Ptatkurapki sensed my frustration, or if it really sensed anything at all. I willfully withdrew from the intercourse, which feat took considerable effort. The image of the Inuit headman faded, and upon opening my eyes, I found myself again sitting opposite an intently glaring bear. To my amazement, and with obviously incredible effort and much facial contortion, the bear began to speak: "I see that you are confused, Rapki." The voice was clear, but so blatantly inhuman that I bristled involuntarily. The bear, or more correctly, Ptatkurapki continued.

"Rapki's souls is one; Ptatkurapki's soul is another. Each is precious and free. Yet here, Rapki must speak for its kind, as Ptatkurapki speaks for *the many*. What does Rapki ask?"

In my most professorial and professional voice, I began. "So, life came to Earth 4.5 billion years ago as the result of *the many* falling to Earth. And some primitive part of *the many* served as the seed from which all life on Earth has now evolved."

At this point the bear interrupted me. "Life came to Earth when the Earth was ready. This thing you call time is an illusion that has no meaning for Ptatkurapki or *the many*. In reality, there is only the beginning and the search."

Perhaps riled by the affront to my scientific accuracy, of more likely by the uncomfortable circumstance of conversing with a bear, my response was short and a bit sarcastic. "The search? The search for what?! Mankind has spent thousands of years trying to understand this world, this life. And the result is that *we* have made some sense of things; have been able to understand the order of things – the *time* and *place* and *method* by which they have occurred, and you tell me *time* has no meaning, that *time* is an *illusion!* Of course it is! An illusion man uses as a tool to understand the relationship between things. Yet, you say it has no meaning for Ptatkurapki or *the many*. Are you saying that man's accomplishments count for nothing?" Whether or not I was originally offended, I certainly constructed the offense as I answered.

For what must have been the next several hours I argued with and harangued Ptatkurapki via the ursine interlocutor with every human accomplishment imaginable, carefully delineating each's importance to the rise of man. After each great flourish I expected some rebuttal, but got none. Increasingly consternated, I finally demanded in as caustic a tone as I could muster: "Say something, dammit! Men have done great things while you've, while Ptatukurapki has done nothing but feed and grow and…and…what? Think?!"

I suppose out of pity for the bear, Ptatkurapki loosed its hold on the beast, and as before, as the light of intelligence faded from its eyes, animal terror returned, with a repeat of the earlier acrobatics and frantic retreat ensued, the animal only looking back over its shoulder occasionally to make sure I was not in pursuit. As before, Ptatkurapki entered my mind, and we continued our conversation there, less the image of the headman. The answers given were simple, and devastating.

"Ptatkurapki has no eyes with which to see. Ptatkurapki has no ears with which to hear. Ptatkurapki has no hands with which to feel. But Ptatkurapki receives and transmits those quantum electromagnetic fluxions that are the essence of thought. And each thought, as an eternal quantum entanglement, is recorded in the very map of Ptatkurapki's soul. Ptatkurapki, and *the many*, are not limited by the physical constraints of Rapki's species, neither struggling to obtain essentials, nor fleeing from adversities. What Ptatkurapki does not accomplish, *the many* will. If Ptatkurapki should perish, there are other ones from *the many* who will flourish. Now, Ptatkurapki prepares for the budding. The mass is gathered; the power of the fusion grows. Soon Ptatkurapki will be *many* again."

Something in this last statement clicked in a very visceral fashion – not as a threat, but cautionary. I quickly surveilled my surroundings, and to my surprise noted that the small island hillock upon which I had landed now comprised an increasingly expansive dome of rising tundra nearly a hundred meters across and twenty or so meters in height above the surrounding terrain. And it was increasing perceptibly! Whatever Ptatkurapki was, it was evident that it was expanding. Again the answers appeared in my mind before the questions were ever formalized.

"Just as the thing called a 'flower' blossoms, and in the blossoming consummates its purpose, the male and the female parts joining to produce the seed of the next generation, so now Ptatukurapki prepares to bud, and in the budding, all that was Ptatkurapki will be written in the DNA of the spores that will burst into the cosmos, there to drift until some new fertile place is encountered."

Perhaps sensing my unease and confusion as recent events unfolded, Ptatkurapki took an entirely unexpected tack. Upon surveying my surrounds in an attempt to gage the rate of change, and perhaps get a sense of when the 'bursting' might take place, my peripheral vision detected a motion. Turning in that direction I saw what appeared to be a distant human figure moving in my direction. My attention remained fixed on the figure for several minutes as it approached, until I was able to make out the traditional garb of the

Inuit. The figure approached the edge of the pool surrounding my now mountainous camp, and stood there, making no sounds or signs. The only way to get across the water was to use the hoverod, so I fired up its thrusters, and set off in the direction of my mysterious guest.

The figure did not move as I approached, only rotating its stance a little so as to face the spot where I landed the hoverod. I quickly dismounted, and nearing the figure was greeted with the smiling face of a young Inuit woman not passed thirty. She obviously noted the bemused and certainly confused expression on my face, to which she responded: "I will go with you," then nodding in the direction of the island. I was at a total loss, so taking her instructions literally, I led her to the hoverod, helped her up onto its platform, and affixed her safety harness. She said nothing more, and at this point I could think of nothing to say, so I fired up the hoverod, and spun it to the direction of my island camp.

Arriving at camp, I settled the hoverod and immediately turned to assist my passenger with her harness. I found her staring at me quite intensely. By now divested on any sense of social decorum, I asked her point blank: "Are you real? Or just another of Ptatkurapki's hallucinations."

She did not seem at all surprised by my question, and answered blithely: "Does it matter?" She then commenced an inspection of my camp, peering closely at each item; handling and turning those items she could.   Emboldened by her nonchalance, I reached out and touched her hand as she held one of the kitchen utensils. She looked at me unsurprised, and smiled. "Are you satisfied?" She ask the question quite gently, kindly, her English pronunciation precise, with only the hint of an aboriginal accent. She slipped the hood of her light, summer amauti back, revealing a beautifully symmetric face – piercing black eyes under pouting epicanthic folds; high, rounded cheekbones; cherubic lips beneath a delicately sculpted nose; all framed by straight ebony hair worn just below the ears and cut straight across at the bangs just above delicately arching brows. The fairness of her skin indicated she did not spend considerable time exposed to the Arctic elements.

Touching the soft warmth of the skin at the back of her hand had sent signals to my brain that screamed reality.   Yet, my recent experiences caused me to doubt even this most convincing tactile encounter. I answered her honestly, though plaintively: "I don't know. I…Right now I can't be certain of what is real and what is put into my mind…"

She interrupted: "…by Ptatkurapki?"

The name came so familiarly to her lips that I reflexed a surprised and confused look, to which she answered: "Yes. I know Ptatkurapki. Like you, I am Rapki. I have known him…err, *it*!... all of my life. At least, all of the life I remember." She turned toward the camp mess, and smiling coquettishly over her shoulder at me, said: "I'm starved!"

CHAPTER 28

The appearance of the young woman had a calming effect on my increasingly agitated state. I imagined Ptatkurapki was in full control of the situation, trying to calm my fears much as a parent soothes an anxious child with a familiar toy.

If the girl *was* a hallucination, it involved all of my senses. Feeling the warmth and softness of the girl's flesh was as convincing as any experience I can recount. And though the headman image was obviously a visual hallucination, I was convinced that mine and Anun's encounters with bears were real experiences, the result of Ptatkurapki controlling the minds of the animals. Particularly, the inhuman quality and obviously excruciating delivery of speech from my ursine interlocutor convinced me that the bear was being manipulated into performing an act of which it was not naturally capable. The fact that that this young woman was hungry greatly assuaged my doubts as to her physical reality, yet I was still left to wonder if she was also being manipulated by Ptatkurapki.

As I conjectured, I responded to her plight. "I don't have much to offer, some rather suspicious hash and some hot coffee."

"That would be wonderful!" she gushed. "A little *muktuk* on the side would be nice!" She grinned mischievously.

I knew the Inuit word for "blubber" from the taunting I had suffered at the hands of the Inuit mine workers. "Sorry, I'm fresh out," I said as I shrugged apologetically.

"No matter. It's not good for my figure!" We both smiled at her humor.

"You must know I have a million questions to ask," I said as I turned to preparing the hash and coffee. She stepped to my side, taking charge of the coffee as I dispensed canned hash into a skillet for heating.

"My name is Anaana." She offered me her hand, which, after clumsily shifting the skillet to my left hand, I accepted. Her hand was warm, and soft, and real.

Knowing that in Inuit society a person's name carries great meaning and importance, I inquired: "What does it mean? Your name – Anaana." I attempted to pronounce it exactly as she had. I saw that she blushed immediately.

In an almost apologetic whisper, she answered: "Beautiful...It is the Inuit word." She looked down, obviously embarrassed.

"If ever a name fit a face..." I offered, but stopped short when I saw that it only caused her cheeks to further redden. "I'm John, John Bander."

"Yes, I know," she rejoined matter-of-factly. Somehow, I was not surprised.

We finished preparing the meal in relative silence, and sitting at the small camp table turned our full attention to making quick work of the hash. Perhaps due to her suggestion, or the kinetic events of the day, I too was possessed of a ravenous appetite. When we had finished, and put away our utensils, Anaana poured us another cup of coffee, and said: "Shall we talk?"

Trying to hold back the torrent, I took my coffee cup, and motioned toward the fire canister. Even in midsummer evenings were chilled at this latitude. The fire would warm us, and as in all ages past, we could share our stories in its glow.

"I suppose it's silly to ask, but are you from around here?" Even my voice sounded silly, with a smattering of aggressiveness. I wanted some answers. "I mean, your English is perfect, and you don't look like you spend a lot of time outdoors. And how in the world did you get here?" I bit my tongue to prevent assaulting her with too many questions at once.

Nonplussed by my rather edgy inquisition, she replied pleasantly: "Shall I start at the beginning?" The look on her face told me she was prepared for an extended narrative. I could only mutter a rather acquiescent: "Sure…"

We spent the next hours telling and comparing our stories. As mine is already known to the reader, I shall dedicate these next paragraphs to telling Anaana's story as it was told to me.

Anaana was the youngest child and only daughter of an Inuit headman whose "village" followed grazing caribou into the surrounding region during summer months. It was his image that Ptatkurapki used in producing my earlier hallucinations. It seems that this headman had experienced interactions with Ptatkurapki, but having no science, and only tradition to guide him, he had attributed his experience to spiritual contacts. It first happened one day as he scouted near the location of the island camp for signs of the wandering caribou. As he told it to his daughter, it had begun as a buzzing in his head, then blossoming into myriad hallucinations of bears and seals and caribou, and great woolly behemoths, giant wolves, and great, fanged cats. As the village Angakkuq, he had taken the visions as signs and warnings. He forbid anyone else to go near to the place.

The headman had returned to the location many times in subsequent years, seeking to commune with the spirits. On one occasion he had taken his young daughter along, thinking that her age and sex isolated her from spiritual contact. Much to his surprise, as they neared the location, but long before he had ever experienced contact, she had tugged at his parka and said: "Ataataga, I hear something!"

The headman had turned in surprise and ask his daughter: "What do you hear, Anaanakuluga?"

Her small eyes opened wide in wonder, she had answered him: "I hear the voices of *anirniit!*"

Flummoxed, the headman chastised his daughter: "Children, *particularly girl children*, don't hear the voices of the spirits!" It was as if by his sternness he meant to dissuade her.

"I do hear them! I do hear them!" She was as insistent as ever. From that day, Anaana assumed a special place in the life of her father, and of her village.

A female Angakkuq was not unheard of among Anaana's people, but in recent times they had become extremely rare. And so certain was this young girl of her ability, and so precise in recounting the things she saw and heard, that her sincerity quickly vanquished all doubt. She became her father's catechumen – he relating the history and shamanic secrets of the people; she absorbing every word.

She admitted to a near obsession with her new found art, always begging her father to take her again to the place of voices and visions. Though the region remained forbidden to the people in general, the headman acquiesced, and he and his mystical young daughter began to make regular sojourns to the "sacred place".

Very often as Anaana unfolded her story before me she would close her eyes and begin to sway gently, the light from the fire canister further accenting her motion. It produced such an otherworldly sensation in me that I was inclined to pinch or slap myself. But not wanting to disturb the flow of her story, I refrained.

Visits to the *place of voices and visions* became a regular ritual for Anaana and her father. Two *qimmiit*, members of the last of the indigenous canine breeds, pulled a lightweight qamutik made from sticks and caribou skin and shaped somewhat like a kayak, that slid easily across the summer vegetation. In it were several day's supply of food, and a small skin tent. Often their visits lasted for a week or more. Though the Inuit are good navigators in the native habitat, they could always count of the dogs to let them know when they were near the sacred site. Long before or Anaana or her father sensed any buzzing in their heads, the sudden fixation of the dogs' attention to a point on the horizon, and their determined and inalterable pace in its direction indicated the place was at hand.

Always the ritual was the same. Upon arriving they would quickly set up their small tent, feed the dogs, and light a small fire in a *kudlik* filled with blubber. In its glow they would eat a simple meal of *mipku*, tearing off pieces of the jerky and chewing it silently until it moistened and dissolved. Then, as the midnight Artic twilight descended and the glow of the Borealis danced higher in the heavens, Anaana and her father would sit on caribou rugs at the entrance of their small tent, starring into the distance, calling forth the spirits with the chants of their people.

If the visions came, they always came first to Anaana. And even when the headman was made party, never did the voices or vision come as strongly as they did to his daughter.

At first the voices and visions would come unheralded, beginning as a slight buzzing in her head and flashes of light in her peripheral vision. Then sounds became distinct and images began to form. They were the sounds and images of things familiar to her – great white bears and wolves and seals and such. But then the figures would morph into things unknown to her at the time, but which she came to know. There were mastodons, giant toothed tigers, giant beaver and sloth, wild pigs and wild horses, all now long gone from her lands. Soon she realized that when questions occurred to her, as quickly some sound or vision appeared in answer. She began to feel that she was truly communicating with something very ancient. She thought it might be the earth itself.

As time passed new and sometimes disturbing and frightening images came to Anaana. Sometimes she was floating lost among the stars. Sometimes she seemed to be on other worlds, with plants and creatures of such incredible form they defied description. Sometimes she found herself looking into the reflected eyes of creatures whose images were at once fantastic and unbelievable, and yet in strange ways incredibly beautiful, whose consciousness and spirits she felt were her own.

And so it went for all the years of her youth. Anaana became so knowledgeable in so many unexplained ways about so many scarcely imaginable things that many in her village thought she was possessed, or had entered the spirit world and had become nothing more than a spirit herself. She was both feared and revered.

Having finished the narrative of her life to this point, the young Inuit woman sitting across the fire from me fell silent, the flames reflecting from the dark, liquid pools of her eyes.

To say that I was bursting with questions at this point would be insufficient. My mind was literally on fire with them, and now given the opportunity, they became a wild and uncontrolled conflagration. They raged forth effortlessly, each leaving me breathless, yet only allowing sufficient time for a concise answer, the next question leaping forth before Anaana's last syllable's vibrations ceased. I will try here to recount the exchanges in as orderly and as journalistic a fashion as I can, recording only my question and her answer, leaving it to the reader to analyze:

Q. This thing, this Ptatkurapki, it's a conscious, living being?
A. As certainly as you are.
Q. It's been here since the beginning?
A. Ptatkurapki brought life to Earth.
Q. Is he – is *it* – the thing we call God?
A. Ptatkurapki is only one of Many.

Q. How did he – *it* – get here?

A. The Rapki, the One, that came before Ptatkurapki, accomplished the Budding, and in so doing burst forth as Ptat, the Many, setting them among the stars to drift forever, or to fall upon a fertile place and take root.

Q. So this word, this sound – Ptatkurapki – means "many from one"?

A. It is a single, reciprocating thought. It is the question and the answer. It is the circle of life, given a single name: *Many from One; One of Many.*

Q. What does it want from me? What does it want from *you?*

A. Ptatkurapki wants nothing. Ptatkurapki records all that is, and in recording all, passes it to the Many.

Q. The multi-helical DNA…it records information in its genetic code?

A. Ptatkurapki *is* the record of all that has been. All of the parts of Ptatkurapki serve to accomplish this.

Q. Can Ptatkurapki answer the scientific questions I have? Does it know how the universe came to be as it is? My kind, our kind – humans - we need so many answers in order to fix the problems that now plague us. Can Ptatkurapki help?

A. Ptatkurapki has no answers. All life struggles to exist.

Q. Doesn't *it* care that there is suffering?

A. Ptatkurapki has recorded that the end of one suffering is but the beginning of another.

Q. Doesn't this *thing* have any feelings? It killed six men with its bioelectricity. Doesn't *it* care?!

A. Ptatkurapki did not kill. Misfortune and electricity killed those six men. Ptatkurapki did not create life; Ptatkurapki has no power over death.

Q. So what's the purpose?! Does this *thing* even HAVE a purpose?! You say it is conscious, that it thinks...what does it *think* about?!

A. Ptatkurapki considers the record it has made. It dreams of things yet to be recorded.

Q. But why? If it's just going to lay there, taking in information, with no intent to act, what meaning does its life have? Billions of years of just laying around collecting data...all that time...what possible sense does it make?

A. Ptatkurapki does not know "time". It knows only what was, what is, and what might be. As for purpose, Ptatkurapki's purpose is the ultimate purpose of all life in the universe – to know the *One* who made us all!

Q. Looking for GOD? You mean its sole purpose, all the budding and gathering and drifting in space, for billions and billions of years - is to *know GOD?*

A. Ptatkurapki cannot create, only pass on the knowledge of what has been created. It can see through the eyes of other living things; it can know what other living things know. It cannot live the life of another living thing. Another living thing cannot live the life of Ptatkurapki. To live and to know – these things are the purpose of Ptatkurapki's existence. Living and knowing are the path to the *One* who made us all.

I was exhausted and frustrated after this exchange, an acrid, metallic taste in my mouth. It was a vicious circle, my every question getting me no closer to the satisfaction I wanted. And all the while, Anaana had given her answers as if reading them from a script, no sign of emotion on her face. I thought to direct a question specifically to the young Inuit woman to escape this cycle.

"Anaana, have I been talking with you, or with Ptatkurapki?" I was not prepared for the answer.

"Ptatkurpaki has been speaking with you through the consciousness of Anaana, one of your kind, whose thoughts as quantum entanglements persist forever and are recorded within Ptatkurapki. Ptatkurapki and the Many know of life in many forms, each form having its own needs. Ptatkurapki has no needs. Either the seed falls where it may grow, or it perishes. The one may be lost, but the many flourish. It is for each kind to find its purpose, and persist, or to lose its faith and perish."

A sudden buzzing returned in my head. The reality that had so convincingly persisted for these past several hours suddenly became illusive. The young Inuit woman before me transmogrified before my eyes, first to an Inuit girl, and then to an Inuit child. A sort of panic set in as I realized that

I had been completely taken in by Ptatkurapki's illusions. Suddenly I found myself sitting alone on the tundra, looking across the water at the figure of a small Inuit girl taking the hand of an Inuit adult – an older man; a headman! They turned from me without a gesture and began walking away, their forms soon being absorbed into the mirage like undulations that began to swallow the reality around me.

I don't know how long I slept, or even if I slept. But suddenly I was aware again, sitting on the tundra in the Artic twilight. The fire canister sat before me, its flame extinguished by the lack of fuel, indicating at least eight hours had passed since I had ignited it. I rose unsteadily to my feet, and surveying my surroundings noted that the small island of tundra I had originally settled on now constitute a massive dome some one hundred meters or so in diameter. The circular pond had been pushed outward, its shallow waters now glowing aquamarine, being illuminated beneath by some unseen source. I became aware of a persistent and seemingly increasing undulation between my feet. Soon the expanding tundra began to fissure here and there as it continued to expand, the same bluish light now issuing from these crevices. Alarms began to go off in my head. Quickly I made for the hoverod. I had no thought but to save myself, leaving the camp to its own fate.

The buzzing in my head returned, and I feared I would again lose track of reality, so once gaining the hoverod, I used the safety harness to lash myself securely, and then hit the emergency return. The hoverod sprang to life under my feet, its computers swinging the craft onto a homeward bearing. I hoped Ptatkurapki would not interfere with its operation.

The buzzing increased to the point that I knew hallucinations would soon ensue. I seated myself on the deck of the hoverod, my back against its forward bulkhead and locking my arms around the harness straps, like an ancient sailor lashing himself to mast so as not to be lost overboard during a gale.

And the hallucinations did come - fast and furious! I suddenly found myself floating in the midst of a great blue orb, filled with a multitude of small, cnidarian like creatures no bigger than a man's hand, each glowing intensely at its center. Instinctively, or perhaps by Ptatkurapki's manipulation, I understood that these were the Many, Ptat, about to be cast upon the face of the heavens. It was the budding, the budding of Ptatkurapki, from whence the one would again become many. I also understood, by virtue of my own intelligence, or the prompting of Ptatkurapki, that all that had occurred during its sojourn on Earth was now safely recorded in the DNA of these seeds, these galactic, perhaps intergalactic, spore.

I also understood, or imagined I understood, that these harbingers of the diversity of life on Earth would now carry that potential to other worlds. As quickly, a question posed itself and was answered: What if one of the many fell onto a world already invested with life? Why, as a small, defenseless organism, incapable of escape, it would be devoured by the first passing predator, or perish and be absorbed by the living surface. For only should it fall onto the barren and fissured surface of an emerging world would it find the material to maintain the fusion that is its spark of life.

All of these thoughts and images came to me, or were given to me in parting. As they began to retreat, and my vision once again returned to what I hoped was *the reality* to which *I* belonged, I immediately noted that the hoverod had covered some several kilometers distance. I also noted that the dome of tundra had continued to increase in size, great fissures opening so that shafts of light emanated profusely from it surface. Then, in what at first seemed a slow, graceful eruption, the dome of tundra burst, and what appeared to be a brilliantly lit column of little stars began to ascend, like a swarm of bees, though gaining speed at an incredible pace.

It was several seconds before the shockwave from the event arrived. It nearly blew me from the hoverod's deck, only my tenacious grip on the harness keeping me for dangling helplessly over the side. The craft pitched and yawed and rolled as it gyros struggled to keep it upright.

The light from the ascending mass lit up the sky and tundra, so that I could see the great dark crater left by the emergence of Ptat, the Many. And then there was the back flow of air to fill the void cause be the force of the eruption that once again almost unsettle me and the hoverod.

The whole event lasted less than minute, I suppose, though a protracted sense of time gave it an impression of slow motion. As quickly as it had begun, the light from the eruption began to dim again, the entire mass of glowing spore having accelerated to such velocity and to such height, and dispersing so rapidly, that they appeared for a moment only as a great, glowing nebula, and then with a twinkle they vanished one by one, like embers from a fireworks fading quickly in a night sky

Epilogue

No *official* record of the event exists, though the great fireball was observed at considerable distance and by a considerable population. But arguments soon arose as to whether it had *ascended* or *descended*. In a scramble to prevent a stampede of the curious, or to panic an already stressed population, the official line soon adopted the latter argument. Astronomical and meteorological experts were lined-up and made their pronouncements in media headlines and on evening news broadcasts: *A cometary body had approached and entered the atmosphere from an unexpected quarter and detonated under the intense heat. The event was so sudden and unexpected that people had been mistaken in their determination of its trajectory. The "fireball" had in fact descended from a point in the northern sky a few degrees of arc from the pole star position, had increased in size and brilliance on it entry into the lower atmosphere, and had detonated at an altitude of approximately 30 kilometers, dispersing in a great fountain of fiery remnants, the shock wave produced creating a substantial crater in the Earth's surface.*

The line was so oft repeated that it became the general mantra, and once implanted in the common psyche resulted in an almost automatic ridicule of any argument to the contrary. Still, there were those who persisted in claiming that the phenomenon had risen as a great, coherent ball of plasma, accelerating to a fantastic speed before dispersing into a myriad of lesser plasmic lights quickly swallowed by the vastness of the night sky. Most of us in this camp generally keep our arguments to and among ourselves, though I have ventured this written account for the curious or conspiracy minded among the population who might bother to read it. I am disavowed by any and all public authority, and avoided by most of my professional colleagues. I do still manage to retain employment with Culverson BioTech, as resource exploration in and immigration to the northern provinces continues unabated, and the need to understand the biological implications remains pertinent.

I seldom meet any of the Culverson's face to face, as my "reputation" is somewhat sullied, but on those occasions when we do occupy the same room, we share a glance at a distance, and a knowing smile. It is enough to sustain me. My dear wife and children suffer some social castigation resulting from their unavoidable association with me, but have taken a sort of pride in being aligned with the "kooky Nanuq of Nunavat", an ever more frequent moniker attached to me.

Anun and I continue to work together on a regular basis, though we are generally silent, communicating only when necessary. We did have one very intense and intimate exchange shortly after my recovery from the trauma suffered during the "budding." It was in my dimly lit hospital room; I was still under the influence of certain pain-relieving medications. Yet, I clearly recall his half-illumined form sitting in a chair at my bedside, his lilting voice revealing the second-hand nature of his English. He told me this:

"Anaana was the name of my mother's father's mother. She was a great and respected shamaness of our people. She foretold the coming changes to our land, and the coming challenges to our people. She talked of a 'spirit' in the tundra with which she communed. She never spoke its name, but only called it the 'seeker.' From it she learned that all of life is a quest to 'know the One that made us All.'"

Anun had fallen silent after these words, and in the shadows sat for a considerable time at my bedside, hands folded on his lap, his head bowed slightly. Though the medication gave an aura of otherworldliness to the moment, my mind raced through the memories of the past days, each moment a clearly framed picture, and yet I could not find the words with which to respond adequately to his revelations. I could only mutter again and again, with increasing emotion: "I know…I know!.....I KNOW!" My final outburst satisfied him, and yet did not disturb his composure. He stood and gently laid a hand upon my languid arm, and patted it several times, like one might pat an injured child to give solace. He left the room quietly, leaving me to wander narcotically through my dreams.

I am forever changed and unsettled by my experience. I can no longer look at my life and its passing days from a pedestrian vantage. I still dedicate my labors to the support of my wife and children, and am as determined as ever to utilize my talents to help my fellow men through the present and coming tribulations. But more often now I seek solitude, and frequently walk along the tundra, beneath the undulating borealis, my thoughts turned to eternity, and whether I shall be a part of it, and like Ptatkurapki, forever seek to know the One that made us All. I marvel at this being, the member of a species so foreign to our own, unfettered by the need to struggle against gravity, to labor for its sustenance – evolved only as mind, its single purpose the very conjecture that drives men mad. I wonder if my species - if I - will join in this eternal quest, or whether in the end I and my kind will merely return to the oblivion from which we seem to have come. And as I walk and wonder, contemplating the meaning of this existence - always I am listening for a voice....